Now that some time has passed, I can say it . . . I never told grown-ups that I wasn't one of them. I've always hidden the truth from them, that deep down I've always been five or six years old. I've hidden my drawings from them as well. But I really want to show them to my friends because, to me, they are memories to be cherished.

Antoine de Saint-Exupéry

Textual variant from the manuscript of *The Little Prince*

For Claude Werth

Edited by Alban Cerisier and Delphine Lacroix
Translated from French by Vali Tamm
All citations/attributions are per *La belle histoire du Petit Prince* (Gallimard)

First U.S. edition, 2018
First published by Éditions Gallimard, Paris
© Éditions Gallimard France, 2013
English translation copyright © 2018 by Houghton Mifflin Harcourt Publishing Company

The Little Prince
Text copyright © 1943, renewed 1971 by Consuelo de Saint-Exupéry
English translation copyright © 2000 by Richard Howard

75th Anniversary

The Little Prince

ANTOINE DE SAINT-EXUPÉRY

* *

The Birth of a Prince

* *

An American Birth
A publishing history of The Little Prince

ALBAN CERISIER
French archivist and historian
specializing in the history of publishing

Antoine de Saint-Exupéry's *The Little Prince,* the most widely translated literary work of the twentieth century, a book whose hero has been dispensing wisdom to children and adults worldwide for three quarters of a century, was first published and read in America, despite having been written by a French author.

In France, *Le Petit Prince* wasn't published until April 1946 by Gaston Gallimard, the longtime editor of Saint-Exupéry. So while American and Canadian readers were able to read the book during the author's lifetime, the French were introduced to it after Saint-Exupéry's widely publicized death, in 1944. Therefore the words of *The Little Prince* held even more gravity and emotion for those French readers first experiencing the book.

This foreign birth of *The Little Prince,* during World War II, is only one of the reasons why the story behind its creation is so intriguing—why it is so much more than just a publishing curiosity. For the book went on to enjoy extraordinary success, a feat that is remarkable indeed for a novella based purely on fantasy. As of today, it has been translated into 270 languages and is firmly anchored in the collective memory of countless cultures. So, one might ask, how did this little monarch capture the attention of such a wide audience?

Since his first book, *Southern Mail,* Saint-Exupéry wrote most of his work outside France, in the seclusion imposed on him by his life as an aviator and airman. *The Little Prince* was no exception, born out of the profound feeling of isolation the

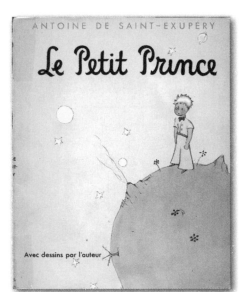

Original French-language edition, New York, Reynal & Hitchcock, 1943.

4

Manhattan, 1940s.

writer experienced while residing in New York City at a time when his friends and countrymen were enduring the horrors of World War II in France. Perhaps the author's need for the guiding hand of a comforting friend was evident even before the publication of the book; its protagonist had already insinuated himself into the writer's life, appearing in the margins of his manuscripts and letters. Sometimes the little prince was winged, in flight; at other times he appeared astride a cloud, or gazing out across vast distances from a high grassy pasture. In whatever form, he was a constant figure within the mental landscape of the exiled poet and pilot. The little prince seemed destined to play two roles there: first, as an ever-present, comforting double of the author—the part of him that still wanted to have faith in the human ability to get along with others; and, second, as someone who, in those dark times when the world was crumbling to pieces, might convey a message of hope to Saint-Exupéry's contemporaries: "Despair," he wrote, "is a very difficult thing. I think I have to be reborn."

When Saint-Exupéry finally embarked on the unique project that would become *The Little Prince,* he dedicated himself to it completely. The book, replete with personal references, was unlike anything he had ever worked on. He illustrated it with his own watercolors and fashioned the little prince in his own image. He wanted his readers to recognize Saint-Exupéry himself in the story through the countless connections between his personal history and the work. He also wanted readers to recognize themselves in it, by awakening their hidden memories of childhood. The result is a narrative infused with a magic and grace that can never be completely grasped.

Antoine de Saint-Exupéry's personal diary, 1943.

"A SINGULAR FRENCHMAN"

In 1943, Saint-Exupéry was already well known among Americans as an author and an aviator. His novel *Night Flight* had been adapted as a film, with Clark Gable in the leading role. The French philosopher Raymond Aron echoed popular sentiments when he described Saint-Exupéry as a "most noble hero, a singular Frenchman."

Saint-Exupéry's frequent crossings of the Atlantic added to his fame: following his first trip to New York, on January 11, 1938, the author made numerous others, at one point making no fewer than five round-trip journeys within a two-year span. Saint-Exupéry also flew within the United States and to South America. On one such flight, to Argentina in 1938, he crashed his Simoun monoplane. He survived but sustained multiple injuries that would be a source of suffering for the rest of his life.

Recuperating in New York, he made final arrangements for the publication of *Wind, Sand and Stars,* the English-language edition of a memoir. This book enjoyed huge success and won the National Book Award. American booksellers marketed *Wind, Sand and Stars* as the best nonfiction publication of 1939. After obtaining special permissions from the French Air Force, Saint-Exupéry embarked on a second trip to New York in 1939, as a second in command to his friend Henri Guillaumet. Saint-Exupéry's glorious past as a mail pilot with the aviation company Aéropostale, combined with his arrival in Long Island aboard the world's largest hydroplane, the *Lieutenant-de-Vaisseau-Paris,* made him even more of a legend. Before the war, he had created a network of professional and personal relationships in New York that he came to lean on for support during his twenty-seven-month wartime exile, from December 1940 until early 1943. His publishers there, Eugene Reynal and Curtice Hitchcock (whom he met in Paris in 1932), and their wives, facilitated his stay; his agent, Maximilian Becker, acted as his intermediary; and his translator, Lewis Galantière, was always available to fine-tune the work of an author who turned it out drop by drop, burying Galantière in endless revisions.

With no shortage of support in New York, Saint-Exupéry returned, despite not speaking a word of English and his misgivings about American society and its "hoards of men in their stone pyramids." On December 21, 1940, he made his sixth transatlantic crossing to the United States, this time from Lisbon, Portugal,

At Rockefeller Center, New York, July 13, 1939.

At the home of the painter
Bernard Lamotte, New York,
about 1941 or 1942.

aboard the SS *Siboney*. He spent the trip in the company of the film director
Jean Renoir, with whom he shared a cabin. The two resembled each other a great
deal, not only physically, but also in their moral and political philosophies. They
reached New York on December 31, 1940. (The two kept in touch throughout
Saint-Exupéry's stay, notably collaborating on a film adaptation of *Wind, Sand
and Stars*. Later, in the spring and summer of 1941, Renoir hosted Saint-Exupéry
at his home in Los Angeles, where the author recuperated from ongoing bouts of
fever and completed his memoir *Flight to Arras*.)

Saint-Exupéry's decision to return was one he had carefully considered in
the months following France's capitulation to Germany, on June 14, 1940. He
had been demobilized on July 31, 1940, and was deeply affected by France's
defeat. He was unsure about what his next move should be, though
he was certain he wouldn't respond to de Gaulle's call to arms to the
French nation from exile in London. Saint-Exupéry cast a wary eye
on France's claim that it had lost a battle, not the war, and on the
country's refusal to take responsibility for its collaboration with the
enemy. He was concerned for the French, who, he felt, had been
taken hostage by German patrols. He claimed that all the armistice
with Germany had accomplished was to save the "essence" of France;
its foundation had collapsed. What was there left to do but plead
with the US government for military intervention?

Once Saint-Exupéry was back at the Ritz-Carlton Hotel in New
York, he reconnected with his closest friends, all of whom, like him,

Antoine de Saint-Exupéry and his friend
Henri Guillaumet, seen from the back,
upon their arrival in New York aboard the
Lieutenant-de-Vaisseau-Paris, July 1939.

Upon arriving in New York aboard the SS *Siboney,* December 31, 1940.

Antoine de Saint-Exupéry with the Reynals, New York, 1941 or 1942.

were expatriates living in the city. Foremost among the group was the painter Bernard Lamotte, in whose home Saint-Exupéry crossed paths with Charlie Chaplin, Marlene Dietrich, Greta Garbo, Jean Gabin, and others. He was also close to Pierre Lazareff, a journalist at the War Information Office, and his wife, Hélène, who worked for *Harper's Bazaar*. In April 1941, *Harper's* ran an interview with Saint-Exupéry, in which he was asked about his favorite books. "The first book I ever loved," Saint-Exupéry confided, "was a collection of fairy tales by Hans Christian Andersen."

His arrival in New York aboard the SS *Siboney* was reported by the *New York Times* in its first issue of 1941 and was followed, two weeks later, by the announcement of his acceptance of the National Book Award for *Wind, Sand and Stars,* belated due to his being in France at the time of the original award in 1939. The ceremony took place before an audience of fifteen hundred at the Astor Hotel. By this time, Saint-Exupéry could tap into his royalties, which allowed him to rent a comfortable apartment at 240 Central Park South, overlooking Central Park. And it was in the Arnold Café, on the ground floor of this building, that, according to some sources, the Reynals first suggested that he write a children's book.

Then, unfortunately, a series of damaging allegations began to surface, claiming Saint-Exupéry had supported the Vichy regime in France. By the end of January 1941, his red carpet had been sullied. These attacks, led by a group that Saint-Exupéry referred to as "the fake French mob in New York," tarnished his stay in New York and

9

A copy of *Terre des Hommes (Wind, Sand and Stars)* with Antoine de Saint-Exupéry's cover, given as a gift to Bernard Lamotte: "After an evening at his house, Bernard Lamotte and I felt that strong sensation of the Earth's rotation (NB, the elephant is in Asia. It balances out our weight, so that the Earth can keep on spinning)."

Bernard Lamotte's desk engraved by Saint-Exupéry and the painter's other guests.

profoundly affected his emotional state. *Flight to Arras,* a powerful memoir of his military involvement in the fight against Nazi barbarism and anti-Semitism, was published in February 1942, but did little to dispel the controversy: his nuanced position of opposing Vichy, but not supporting de Gaulle, was problematic among New York's French diaspora, who rallied to de Gaulle's cause. Saint-Exupéry was depressed, beset by a gnawing sense of guilt and vulnerability. He paced about futilely in exile, where, despite his friendships and romantic entanglements, he felt cramped.

But he was no Alphonse de Lamartine, the French romantic poet who, in his poem "Isolation," wrote: "One sole being is missing and the world is a desert / Why do I stay in this land of exile? / I share nothing in common with this Earth." According to Saint-Exupéry, it is precisely in the experience of the desert, of dunes and clouds, of icebergs and skyscrapers, that a person feels the true presence of the self and our fellow humans. Even in his lowest moments, he never gave in to despair. His long meditations on his birthplace and frequent retreats into childhood memories unveiled for him the hidden struggle of being alive. He came to perceive, in the sky's whispers and the twinkling of a star, something spiritual: the absent and the regretted, the abandoned and the missing. Against this backdrop, the little prince—that companion in exile, whose interstellar adventures bear witness to these revelations with grace, gravity, and simplicity—took shape.

*

"THE ONLY TRUTH IN LIFE"

We don't really know who should be credited with the idea for *The Little Prince.* Both the Hitchcocks and the Reynals claimed this honor in interviews late in their lives, as did Silvia Hamilton, one of the writer's New York companions. The painter Hedda Sterne remembered encouraging the author to illustrate the book himself. Each of these people claimed that their friend's obsessive drawing of expressive little characters led them to suggest that he turn them into the hero of a children's book. So it was no surprise that this idea came to fruition, or that the author's American publisher gave the project its blessing. After all, it was under the Reynal & Hitchcock imprint that Pamela Lyndon Travers's *Mary Poppins* first

Saint-Exupéry and his American editors, prior to the publication of *Wind, Sand and Stars*, July 1939.

appeared in the States (later, Travers would write a rave review of *The Little Prince* for the *New York Herald Tribune;* it appeared on April 11, 1943).

Of course, possibly it was Saint-Exupéry himself who came up with the idea of writing a children's story, for he held the genre in the highest esteem. In his *Letters to a Stranger,* he wrote: "We know all too well that fairy tales are the only truth in life."

There's also a whole parade of friends, including Paul-Émile Victor and René Clair, who remembered offering him boxes of watercolor pencils and gouaches for the first sketches. In the end, however, the writer saw to this need himself by buying his own supplies in an Eighth Avenue drugstore.

Saint-Exupéry set about working on the project at the beginning of the summer of 1942 (the letters he wrote from Montreal during the month of May made no allusion to *The Little Prince*). Summer and fall were devoted to the composition of the story and its drawings. Several testimonials support this timetable, chief among them that of Consuelo de Saint-Exupéry, his wife since 1931. She arrived in New York on November 6, 1941, and had soon installed herself in her own apartment at 240 Central Park, close to her husband's. The couple had already been living separately for several years, and Saint-Exupéry's lifestyle in New York wasn't conducive to fostering a deeper connection: the marital relationship was tempestuous at best.

During this time, Silvia Hamilton, Hedda Sterne, Nada de Bragance, and Nathalie Paley were sources of solace for the author, if not maternal figures. While at Silvia's home during the

At Silvia Hamilton's house, under the watchful gaze of a doll with a mop of golden hair.

This Agreement,

made this   26th day of January, 1943   x193x

by and between   Antoine de Saint-Exupéry, 35 Beekman Place, New York, New York
party of the first part, the Author   and/or Proprietor   (hereinafter in either case termed "the Author   "),
and REYNAL & HITCHCOCK, Inc., of 386 Fourth Avenue, New York, N. Y., party of the second part
(hereinafter termed "the Publisher").

The Author   declares that   he   is the sole proprietor   of this work and that   he has   full power
to make this agreement.

In consideration of the premises and of the promises hereinafter set forth, it is agreed by the parties
hereto as follows:

1.   (a)   The Author   hereby grants and assigns to the Publisher the sole and exclusive right to publish
in book form   in the English and French languages throughout the world including
Canada but excepting the balance of the British Empire which shall be lft to the
Author, his new book entitled THE LITTLE PRINCE, written and illustrated by the
Author, the English translation thereof having been arranged by the Publisher.

(b)   The Author   also grants to the Publisher such other rights as are set forth in Clause 16
hereof.

2.   (a)   It is understood and agreed that the copyright shall be taken out by the Publisher at his own
expense in the name of the Author   or of the Publisher in the United States of America.   In the event
that said work has been or will be published abroad prior to American book publication, the Author   agrees
to place a copy of the foreign edition of said work in the hands of the Publisher in ample time to protect such
American copyright.

(b)   The Author   agrees to make timely application for the renewal of the said copyright within
one (1) year before the expiration of the copyright therein.

3.   The Author   hereby guarantees that the said work is in no way a violation of any existing copyright
either in whole or in part, and that it contains no matter which, if published, will be libellous or otherwise
injurious; and that   he   will, at   own expense, protect and defend the said work from any adverse
claims that said work infringes any copyright, and   he   will indemnify and save harmless the Publisher from
all damages, costs and expenses arising by reason of any alleged injurious or libellous matter in the said work.

4.   The Author   agrees to deliver the manuscript copy of the said work to the Publisher on or before
Delivered   in proper shape for the press.   Time is of the essence of this agreement; and if
delivery be not made on or before the stipulated date, the Publisher shall not be bound by the time limit for
publication provided in Clause 6; and if within three (3) months after written notice from the Publisher to
the Author   or   representative, said delivery be not made by the Author   , this shall be
deemed cause for the Publisher, if he so desires, to terminate this agreement (and to recover from the
Author   any and all amounts which he may have advanced to the Author   as hereinafter provided).   The
Author   further agrees to supply promptly all photographs, drawings, charts or index if such be necessary
to the completion of the said manuscript, and if he fails to do so, the Publisher shall have the right to supply
them and shall charge the cost thereof against any sums accruing to the Author   under this agreement.

5.   The Author   agrees, upon the request of the Publisher, to read, revise and correct and promptly
return all proof sheets of the work, and to pay in cash or, at the option of the Publisher, as a charge against
any sums accruing to the Author   under this agreement, the cost of alterations in type or in plates,
required by the Author   , other than those due to printer's errors, in excess of ten percent (10%) of the
original cost of composition, provided a statement of these charges be mailed to the Author   within thirty
(30) days after the receipt of the printer's bills, and the corrected proofs be presented for the inspection of
the Author   at the office of the Publisher, upon the former's request therefor.

6.   The Publisher agrees to publish the said work at his own expense within
after the date of receipt by him of the complete manuscript copy thereof, on or before   May 1, 1943
in such style and manner as he shall deem best suited to its sale; but this limit, in case of strikes or other
non-preventable delays or in case the Author   fails to return proofs within thirty (30) days after he has
received them, shall be extended to cover such delays.   Should the Publisher fail to publish the said work
before the expiration of said period, except as provided herein in Clause 4, the Author   shall have the
right to make written demand on the Publisher for such publication and if the work shall not be published
within sixty (60) days after receipt of such demand, the Author   shall have the right to terminate this
agreement on repayment of any moneys advanced to   him   on account of this contract or ex-
pended by the Publisher toward publication.

Contract for the American publication of *The Little Prince,* January 26, 1943.

With Silvia Hamilton's poodle, presumed model for the sheep, 1942.

second half of 1942, Saint-Exupéry found some of the prototypes upon which he modeled the characters of *The Little Prince:* a doll with a mop of golden hair, a little poodle that looked like a sheep, and Hannibal, Silvia's pet boxer, which turned out to be a perfect model for the tiger!

Outfitted with his box of painting supplies and his Dictaphone, and accompanied by his personal secretary, Saint-Exupéry set to work on his project in Bevin House, a mansion in Asharoken, on the northeast coast of Long Island. Consuelo had found the place at the end of the summer of 1942 and rented it to shield her husband from the summer heat wave, and from his impassioned conflicts with his fellow expats in the city. He apparently liked it there, at least according to his writer friends Denis de Rougemont and André Maurois, who were part of a steady stream of visitors that also included Adèle Breaux (see page 33), his English-language tutor. He used these friends as models for his sketches and solicited their suggestions at all hours of the night. He also took advantage of the three-hour time difference between the East and West Coasts of the United States to consult by phone with his friend the actor Annabella Power in Los Angeles late into the night.

Bevin House in Asharoken, Long Island, where Saint-Exupéry wrote *The Little Prince* at the end of the summer of 1942.

Eventually, however, Saint-Exupéry began to distance himself from this "house of happiness." It had begun to feel confining, much like a very small planet. He began to sneak off to the city, or to Washington, DC. By mid-October, he had submitted the manuscript of *The Little Prince* to Curtice Hitchcock, who quickly conveyed his approval to Maximilian Becker, Saint-

Exupéry's agent. The contract for American publication was signed with Reynal & Hitchcock: the publisher would produce editions in both English and French.

In December, the Saint-Exupérys settled into a duplex apartment at 35 Beekman Place in New York, where they enjoyed a lull in their marital troubles. When Consuelo was assaulted on an outing near there, Antoine wrote to his friend Silvia, confessing, "I suddenly feel intensely responsible for her, like a captain for his ship."

✳

"I KNOW PRECISELY WHICH DRAWING I WANT WITH THIS TEXT"

The writer had put his heart and soul into his work. The countless sketches he produced at the time testify to this fact. Each of his final drawings was executed to perfection.

Despite his tireless work, the book was not published fast enough to please Saint-Exupéry. He expressed his frustration in a letter to his American editor, complaining that Becker's unwanted interference was causing delays. In the same letter, he also reminded the publisher of the way he wanted to handle the layout of the pages: "Above all, I want to make it clear that, where any decisions are to be made, it is I who will decide on a) the placement of illustrations, b) their relative dimensions, c) whether or not they should be in full color, and d) how the captions should read. So, where I write, for example . . . 'this is the best drawing I've been able to make of him,' I know precisely which drawing I want to accompany this text, whether I want it to be large or small, in color or in black and white, and embedded within the text or stand-alone." This attention to detail is reflected in the final manuscript of *The Little Prince;* the written word and the illustrations are inextricably linked.

Saint-Exupéry's frustration with the publication delay is also captured in another letter. To Annabella Power he wrote about a singularly beautiful paperback edition of *The Little Prince* he had sent her. He explained, "The reason I am so late in sending this to you is that I couldn't possibly send you the text without the illustrations, and it took the publisher a full four months to reproduce them (they are so beautiful . . .)." The title of that volume was in English, and included the only printing sheets that integrated the full-color drawings with both the French and English texts.

Although Saint-Exupéry may have been justified in his frustration over the

Manuscript pages from *The Little Prince.*

time it took for his work to be published, a possible explanation was the fact that his translator, Lewis Galantière, had been injured in a plane accident. Saint-Exupéry visited him in the hospital in January 1943, bringing him two drawings (see pages 66 and 67) and a typewritten version of his text as a gift. These are now held in collections in Austin, Texas. Following the accident, Katherine Woods, a new translator, jumped in and took over the job.

Notably, the author didn't revise the text much from the version he had originally submitted to the publisher. The original manuscript, now in the Morgan Library & Museum in New York, does show some variations (for example, it omits an explicit reference to Manhattan and descriptions of visits to a New York shop and to a prominent engineer and inventor, as well as digressions on the inherent beauty of hills), but the published version was not materially different from the original submitted. Three of the five typewritten drafts of the text known to exist today contain the author's handwritten corrections, none of which amounted to significant changes. One of them, which Saint-Exupéry gave as a gift to the pianist Nadia Boulanger, is now in the French National Library (see pages 64 and 65).

One other version of the work, however, sheds an interesting light on its trajectory from manuscript to published book. A little-known set of corrected proofs of the American French edition was printed single-sided and given by the author to his friends Tyrone and Annabella Power. In this copy, the text is laid out on the pages, with spaces left for the illustrations. It provides two key pieces of information: One concerns the title, which didn't appear in the famous script typeface we are familiar with today, but in a much more classic font, with serifs. This

The Book Saint-Exupery Left Behind

Antoine de Saint-Exupéry, New York, 1942.

Saint-Exupéry poses for the New York press, 1942.

suggests that the decision to use a childlike typeface was made at a later stage, and implies a rethinking of the book's ultimate audience: should it be marketed as a children's story or as a parable for adults?

The second intriguing fact related to this set of corrected proofs is that it included neither the dedication to Léon Werth nor the story's final page, both of which appeared in the published edition. Nor does there seem to be any space reserved for them. Léon Werth (1878–1955) was a Jewish art critic and essayist, a man of profoundly leftist and anti-military convictions and a close friend of the author's in France. When Saint-Exupéry went to the States, leaving behind the menacing anti-Semitic climate created by the German authorities and the Vichy government, Werth entrusted him with a manuscript—a memoir of his June 1940 escape from Paris to the Jura Mountains—so that Saint-Exupéry might compose a preface for it and have it published in New York. The preface was finally published as a stand-alone work in 1943, under the name *Letter to a Hostage* (Werth's name was excised as a precaution); it constitutes one of the most affecting meditations ever written on the isolation and loneliness experienced by exiles. Werth's memoir would be published decades later under the title *33 Days*.

The fact that Saint-Exupéry chose to frame *The Little Prince* with a dedication and epilogue that specifically referenced his friend Werth, the little boy he once was, and the difficult conditions in which Werth, a Jew, now found himself in Nazi-occupied France, is meaningful because it appears that the book was origi-

16

nally supposed to be dedicated to Consuelo. Had the author followed through with this first plan, the dedication would have imparted a completely different flavor to the book. This last-minute change casts the story in a different light and places it in a historical context with a whole new suite of undertones.

Saint-Exupéry's feelings about the war were so strong that he desired nothing more than to enlist again: "My biggest mistake is living in New York while my compatriots are at war and are dying." His wish was finally granted in February 1943, when he was mobilized to Algiers with the Free French Air Force after Allied forces had ousted the Vichy regime, giving them strategic access to southern Europe. He was to depart hastily for North Africa.

During a farewell dinner that Saint-Exupéry gave at Beekman Place, he gathered his guests in his study and read them the manuscript of *The Little Prince* from beginning to end. But the book's publication date had been delayed once again, this time until the spring.

✳

"I HAVE NO IDEA WHAT IS GOING ON WITH *THE LITTLE PRINCE*"

The author's exasperation with the delays in the book's publication did not end after he had left the United States. On June 8 he wrote Curtice Hitchcock from Oujda, Morocco, complaining, "I have no idea what is going on with *The Little Prince,* I don't even know if it has been released yet. I am completely in the dark! Please write me." On August 3, he received a reply: "*The Little Prince* has been met with enthusiasm from children and adults, alike; reviews have been positive. I'm enclosing a few so you can see for yourself. We've already sold almost 30,000 copies of the English edition, and 7,000 of the French, and sales are continuing at a pace of 500–1,000 copies per week despite the summer heat waves."

It seems likely, then, that the reason Saint-Exupéry had not been able to participate in the book's launch was simply that he had left the States before it was ready. This is how his first biographer, Pierre Chevrier (pen name of Nelly de Vogüé, who had been the author's close companion during the 1930s and 1940s), summed it up in 1949: "*The Little Prince* first appeared in bookshops on April 6th. Saint-Exupéry was not able to share in its success firsthand, because at that time he was already aboard an American convoy headed for North Africa." The April 6 publication date is evidently correct because on that same day the *New York Times* featured the title in its "Books Published Today" section. That same issue also featured John Chamberlain's rave review of the book.

However, this scenario doesn't square with official accounts of the author's last few days in New York. These allege that the author left for North Africa sometime between April 11 and April 20. Some have him leaving on a submarine, but it is more likely he departed aboard an ocean liner that had been moored in New York Harbor and then became part of a convoy of about thirty ships bringing troops to Algeria (a voyage Saint-Exupéry himself later wrote about). The date of his departure varies from one biographer to another, however, and the discrepancy is problematic.

Experts rely on entries in the philosopher Denis de Rougemont's diary, which were published in *Icare,* a French aviation publication. The entry dated April 1, 1943, reads: "Consuelo called me this morning to tell me that Tonio will be at her house for lunch and that I should stop by if I want to say goodbye to him." It goes on to describe how Denis went to the Beekman Place apartment with Pierre Lazareff and Roger Beaucaire, and found the writer posing in his uniform for *Life* magazine. That same day the author granted Maximilian Becker power-of-attorney to manage, in his absence, all decisions concerning the book. Before the day was out, according to various accounts, the author paid a visit to Hitchcock at his house, dined at the home of the engineer Jean Mercier, and swung by Hedda Sterne's before returning to Beekman Place in the early hours of the morning. At seven o'clock on the following morning he was at the home of Silvia Hamilton, where he had gone to say goodbye and to give her his camera and a manuscript of *The Little Prince,* the same one now conserved at the Morgan Library & Museum in New York. He was never to see any of these people again: he went missing during his flight of July 31, 1944.

Curiously, this sequence of events is often described as having occurred several days after *The Little Prince* first appeared in bookstores. This timeline is supported by accounts given by people who saw Saint-Exupéry after these events, including the New York psychoanalyst Henry Elkin. Elkin claims to have been on the same liner with Saint-Exupéry, where he befriended the author during his last crossing of the Atlantic. "To the best of [his] memory," they cast off on "April 20th, 1943, or soon thereafter," to reach Oran on May 3 [*Écrits de Guerre* (*Wartime Writings*), *1939–1944,* p. 253]. Elkin added that at the time of their voyage, Saint-Exupéry had in hand a copy of the work "that his publisher had printed in a great rush so that he would have a copy to take with him, before the official print run and before it was put on the market."

Stacy Schiff, Saint-Exupéry's American biographer, tells us that Saint-Exupéry traveled aboard the *Stirling Castle,* a British ocean liner used as a troopship during the war. The arrival and departure records of the port of New York for 1943 have the *Stirling Castle* casting off on April 2, 1943, and traveling as part of convoy UGF7, which carried close to fifty thousand men. She reached Gibraltar on April 12 and Oran, on the northwest coast of Algeria, on April 13. It is of course possible that the author joined a different convoy in the end—for example, the one that left either New York or Baltimore on April 14, 1943, and reached Bône, in eastern Algeria, on May 7 (UGS-7A). Another set of accounts suggests this scenario; several people remembered accompanying the author to the train station. François Evrard, editor of *Wartime Writings, 1939–1944,* interprets Saint-Exupéry's statement "I have no idea what is going on with *The Little Prince*" as referring to the French edition of the book, not the English one.

Saint-Exupéry could have left the United States on April 2, 1943, before the publication of *The Little Prince.* This would perhaps explain the anxious letter he wrote to his publisher and why he had only a single copy of the French edition of his book—insofar as it was bound slightly later than the English-language version. It is hard to imagine, however, that he would not have brought one or two copies of the English-language version with him, as these would surely have been available. They had been picked up from the bookbinders prior to April 2: according to Anne Morrow Lindbergh's journal, she received a copy on March 29, 1943. And, moreover, Saint-Exupéry autographed several copies before he left. Dorothy Barclay, an assistant working for the *New York Times* who had phoned the Hayden Planetarium for Saint-Exupéry to answer his question of just how many stars are visible from Earth, was given an autographed copy. And among book collectors, it is well known that the author signed every single one of the 785 first-printing copies (see page 26). It is possible, of course, that he autographed the books before they were bound.

A *New York Times* article of April 17, 1943, also hints at a departure in early April. The following lines appeared in it: "Antoine de Saint-Exupéry, who, by the time this article has been published, will probably have already reached his overseas destination, has taken up active service again as Captain in the ranks of the French Air Force. Readers of *The Little Prince* will be happy to know that 'Saint-Ex' has taken along a box of watercolors just in case he should cross paths with his little prince . . ."

Advertisement for the US edition of *The Little Prince,* 1943.

Original edition of *The Little Prince,* with a dedication to Dorothy Barclay: "You'd have to be a complete fool to choose to live on this planet; it's not nice here, except at night when the people who live here are all sleeping (the little prince) / the little prince was mistaken. There are certain people on Earth whose honesty, whose kindness and generosity make up for the greediness and selfishness of all the others. Dorothy Barclay, for one."

The history of this book's publication, then, is part foreign birth, part yearning for the innocence of childhood, and part race against the clock, because when Saint-Exupéry left the States, the book he left behind was a part of himself. He was torn between confidence about the delightful and transformative power of his little monarch's words and character, and wariness that unknown forces might smother or disfigure them. This concern would prove needless.

✶

INSPIRATION

Saint-Exupéry drew so heavily from his own experiences when he wrote that countless possible sources of inspiration can be cited, such as his plane crash of December 1935 in the Libyan desert and the subsequent long desert trek, his flights over the Andes, the volcanoes of Consuelo's native El Salvador, the hidden treasures of the houses where he spent his childhood (in Saint-Maurice-de-Rémens in Ain, La Mole, in Provence), and the strong influence of his mother. We also know that the figure of the rose owes much to the disposition of his wife, Consuelo, and their tempestuous relationship.

Literary sources are numerous as well, chief among them the reservoir of fairy tales and their primordial truths. Other influences include *The Lamplighter* (1854), by Marie Cummins, and André Maurois' *The Country of Thirty-six Thousand Wishes* (1929), a copy of which was given to Saint-Exupéry by the author. The scholar Denis Boissier has also detailed the strong parallels between *The Little Prince* and Tristan Derème's *Patachou* (1929; the rose, the stars, the boa constrictor, the fox, the sheep . . .), making the case that the former is an offshoot of the latter. The historian Anne Renonciat disagrees with this interpretation and has argued that, on the contrary, the themes of *The Little Prince* (notably, a yearning for a return to simplicity and transparency) are common to the writer's era, and indeed defined it. Another possible source not to be overlooked is the first public reading of *Man of the Pampa* given by the Uruguayan-born French poet Jules Supervielle. The poet opened this reading, in which volcanoes figured heavily, with these lines, whose echo is heard in *The Little Prince:* "Dreams and reality, farce, anguish. I wrote this short story for the child I once was, the child who asks me to tell him a story."

Possible source of inspiration for Saint-Exupéry's migration of wild birds? A flying machine, from *The Man in the Moone*, by Francis Godwin, London, 1638.

✳

THE LITTLE PRINCE HERE ON EARTH

Because *The Little Prince* was published in France after Saint-Exupéry's death, and because the French publisher didn't have access to the original drawings (they had been left behind in the States) when the book was first published there in 1946, it was illustrated with commissioned watercolors. These reproductions of the author's original work, while not precise copies, were faithful to it. Saint-Exupéry's own artwork was reintroduced in a pocket-size edition in 1999, making the same version of the book available to readers worldwide.

The book was an instant hit in France, surging in popularity in the 1970s. By 2013, more than 11 million copies had been sold. Paris was the springboard for numerous translations: between 1946 and 2000 the book appeared in about twenty new languages and dialects per decade. And while the book enjoyed its greatest fame in Europe until around 1955, it was also becoming popular in far-flung places such as South America—especially in Argentina and Brazil, both of which had connections with Saint-Exupéry—and Japan. In Eastern Europe,

Cartoon by Moebius,
Le Figaro, 2006.

it was just becoming well known during the 1950s and 1960s, though the Communist regime in Hungary banned it in 1957 as unsuitable reading material for young Hungarians:

> This book may spoil the tastes of our children. We live under a socialist regime and this system requires that our children, who are the people of tomorrow, keep both feet on the ground. Nothing should distort the image they must have of life and the world. In order to achieve this, it is not enough to only spare them the stupidity of religious education. When they turn their heads to the skies, they should not look for God and angels, but for Sputniks. Let's preserve our children from the poison of fairy tales like the absurd and morbid nostalgia of *The Little Prince* which yearns so foolishly for death.

The book has also been adapted many times for film, stage, audio, opera, and ballet, and has been published in the form of graphic novels as well. The actor and director Orson Welles was so touched by the story when he first read it, in 1943, that he wanted to adapt it for film. His plan failed because he was unable to win Walt Disney's support—but the Rosebud in his *Citizen Kane* and the rose in *The Little Prince* have a lot in common!

The first film adaptation of *The Little Prince* (1967) was made by the Lithuanian filmmaker Arünas Zebrünas, followed in 1974 by a musical directed by Stanley Donen and produced by Paramount Pictures. In the 1970s, a film adaptation based loosely on the original was released in Japan, and in 1979, Will Vinton adapted the book as a stop-motion Claymation film.

On the basis of the latter, Aton Soumache's production company, Method Films, produced an animated television series in 2011. And in 2015, Mark Osborne, director of *Kung Fu Panda,* teamed up with the graphic artists Hugo Pratt and Joann Sfar to pay homage to Saint-Exupéry's work with a wide-screen animated film adaptation.

From ballet, to opera, to musicals, between 1980 and 2000, a seemingly endless number of *Little Prince* adaptations was produced worldwide. Of particular note are a French stage version by Virgil Tănase (2006), an opera by the Briton Rachel Portman first performed in Houston, Texas (written to an English libretto by Nicholas Wright, 2003), an opera by the Austrian composer Nikolaus Schapfl (2006), and another by the French composer Michaël Lévinas (2017).

In addition, traditional public readings of the book have left their mark on audiences everywhere.

Perhaps, in the end, the broad appeal of *The Little Prince* across languages and interpretations must be seen as a direct reflection of Saint-Exupéry's own persona.

The publication in 2010 of his *Letters to a Stranger,* addressed in 1943–44 to a woman with whom he had fallen in love, is testimony to the fact that, by that time, the author and the protagonist of his book had become one. He even signed his letters by drawing the little prince's face and signature scarf. And whenever the writer was doubtful about his work, or failed to receive replies to his letters, he would use that time to sketch a little princess so that he might continue savoring the story. It was no longer possible to distinguish between the author and his hero, between life and the story he carved out of it, between the world as we know it and the world he created.

For more on the history of *The Little Prince,* see *Il était une fois... Le Petit Prince (Once upon a time there was... The Little Prince),* Gallimard, 2006, as well as the works of Michel Autrand, Michel Quesnel, Stacy Schiff, Virgil Tănase, and Alain Vircondelet, and special issues of the publication *Icare.*

An Unpublished Chapter

Although the author's changes to the final manuscript were minimal, earlier drafts reveal a number of edits. This is the case, for example, with the manuscript now in the Morgan Library & Museum in New York, and with the two autographed, handwritten draft pages of *The Little Prince* that were sold at public auction in Paris on May 16, 2012. These reveal differences in the contents of Chapters XVII and XIX, and include a passage in which the little prince meets a man who has been stumped by a crossword puzzle, a scene omitted from the published edition.

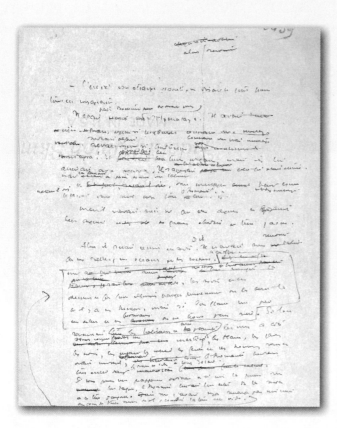

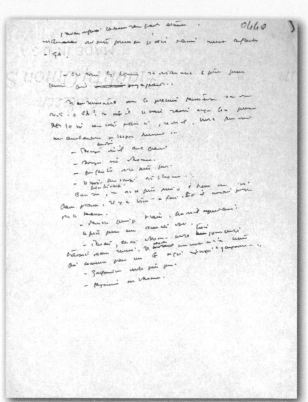

"This is a strange planet," the little prince said to himself as he went on walking. He had set out from the desert and headed directly for the Himalayas. He had wanted to see a true and proper mountain for so long! Because, even though he had three volcanoes of his own, they only came up to his knees. He often used the one that was extinct as a stepstool, but it scarcely made him any taller. "From a tall mountain such as this one," he had said to himself, "I'll be able to see all of mankind at once." But all he could see was some sharp peaks of granite and some yellowish boulders. If one gathered together all the inhabitants of this planet, and stood them next to one another, all packed tightly together as is the case in some big public assemblies, the whites, yellows, and blacks, the children, old people, and all the men and women, without forgetting a single one, all of humanity would fit on . . . Long Island. Or if you took a globe and stuck a pushpin in it, the size of the pinhole would represent the space it would take to house all the people in the world. Of course, after three years of flying planes, I'd already realized on my own how empty Earth is. The roads and railroads you see when looking down on Earth are a little misleading because, though they look like they cover a lot of territory, they're just paths along which humanity is concentrated: the moment you move away from them all that's left is isolation.

But I'd never really thought about that before. It's thanks to the little prince that I started to. "Where are all the people?" the little prince asked himself as he traveled on. Then he met a person along a road. "Ah!" he said to himself. "I'm going to find out what he thinks about life on this planet. This one may be an ambassador of the human spirit."

"Hello," he said to him, cheerfully.

"Hello," said the man.

"What are you doing?" said the little prince.

"I'm very busy," said the man.

"Of course he is very busy," the little prince said to himself, "he lives on such a large planet. There must be so much to do to take care of it." And he scarcely dared disturb him. "Perhaps I can help you," he nevertheless said aloud. The little prince would have enjoyed being helpful.

"Perhaps," the man replied. "I have been working for three days without success. I am looking for a six-letter word that starts with a *G* and means 'gargling.'"

Five hundred and twenty-five copies of the first edition of
THE LITTLE PRINCE
have been autographed by the author, of which
five hundred are for sale. This is
copy number

First Editions

THE FIRST AMERICAN EDITIONS
(IN ENGLISH AND FRENCH)

The first English-language edition of *The Little Prince,* published by Reynal & Hitchcock in New York, on April 6, 1943, consisted of 525 autographed copies (of which 25 were not for sale), each numbered by hand. The publisher's address in those editions was listed as 386 Fourth Avenue. Reynal & Hitchcock's first French-language edition consisted of 260 copies (of which 10 were not for sale), also numbered by hand and signed by the author. Both versions were hardbound, with a salmon-tan linen cloth cover featuring an embossed illustration and protected by a dust jacket that featured a color reproduction of the illustration. And both versions had the 1943 copyright notice. The last page of the English-language edition also had a colophon. On page 63 of the French edition, the illustration of the little prince perched atop a mountain had a macula (a printing fault) located midway up the right-hand side of the leftmost peak. Bibliophiles have christened this the "mark of the raven." By the sixth printing of the French-language edition, this mark had disappeared altogether.

The first mass-market hardcover editions in both French and English differed from the first edition in the color of the linen cloth cover, and in the fact that they didn't list a print run and weren't signed by the author. They were also released as jacketless paperback editions.

Editions of the book printed between 1943 and 1950 included the print run in the line immediately following the copyright notice ("First printing," "Second printing," and so on). In total, there were five printings, numbered 2 to 6, for the English-language edition, and six printings, numbered 2 to 7, for the French edition. In the fifth printing of the English edition and the sixth printing of the French edition, the publisher's address changed from 386 Fourth Avenue to West Eighth Street, and in the seventh printing of the French edition, it changed yet again to 383 Madison Avenue. A Canadian version of the first printing appeared in 1943 and carried the publisher's name as "Beauchemin—Montreal / Reynal & Hitchcock, New York."

The commercial value of these editions varies according to their condition. The signed first edition, complete with its jacket, was valued from $25,000 to $30,000 in 2013. The first mass-market editions are valued at ten times less than that figure, and the value of subsequent print runs is as low as $250.

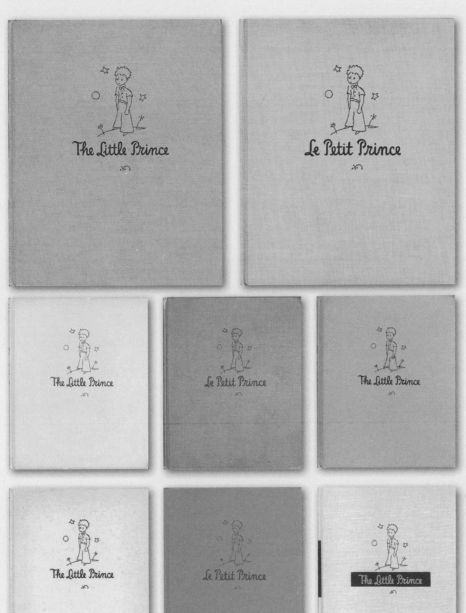

From left to right, top to bottom: original English and French editions, 1943; second English and French editions; third edition; fourth edition; sixth edition; the 1970 edition.

First Editions

THE FIRST EDITION PUBLISHED IN FRANCE

The first printing of *Le Petit Prince* released in France by Gallimard, in April 1946, consisted of 12,750 copies, of which 30 were numbered from I to XXX and were not for sale. This hardcover edition was bound in blue linen cloth and featured an embossed illustration much like the one for the US publication. The logo "nrf" (the letters are taken from *La Nouvelle Revue française;* Gallimard is an offshoot of this literary journal) appeared on the cover and title page, and the book was protected by a full-color illustrated dust jacket (see opposite). Each page consisted of twenty-nine lines (as opposed to the twenty-six lines of the US version). The copyright notice, dated 1945, appeared on the back of the title page, along with a list of the author's other works (curiously, *Night Flight* was not included). The colophon, which was immediately followed by a serial number printed in orange, read: "Printed by / Paul Dupont, Paris / November 30, 1945 / Printing no. 569 / Edition no. 437 / Legal deposit: 4th trim 1945."

This edition contained several misprints and imperfections (mistakes, dashes within numbers, the *o* missing from *œ*). The main differences between this edition and the US edition, which is used as a standard, are listed below:

French-language American Edition, 1943		Gallimard Edition, 1946
Title page	Avec dessins par l'auteur	Avec les dessins de l'auteur
p. 1	Mon dessin numéro 1	mon premier dessin
p. 16	l'astéroïde 325	l'astéroïde 3251
p. 35	à ce que sa autorité	à ce que son autorité
p. 53	faire	farie

The typos in the 1946 edition were corrected in the second edition, with the notable exception of the asteroid number, which was "3251" in the Paris publication and "325" in the New York edition. This typo was not corrected until 1999. But one other mistake managed to slip in starting in the 1950s, and that was the number of sunsets the little prince claimed to have witnessed: it was "43" in the original version, and "44" in editions published from 1950 on. Judging from the typewritten pages known to exist, Saint-Exupéry himself struggled with this number.

The first French paperback edition was published on November 12, 1947; the first edition in a binding designed by Paul Bonet was published on November 30, 1950. Between 1945 and 1996 there was a total of thirty-two printings.

Reflections and Remembrances
Saint-Exupéry's Friends and Family

Consuelo and Antoine
de Saint-Exupéry.

CONSUELO DE
SAINT-EXUPÉRY
Antoine de Saint-Exupéry's wife

You are a true magician where beauty is concerned, and you can be such a good influence on those around you. You teach them how to love life even though you, yourself, find man's company so difficult. He needs so much molding, you feel; you'd prefer to see him be more pure, self-assured. [. . .] I, for my part, am glad to join you in your struggles, whether they be in the desert, or on one of your planes. It hasn't always been all that easy, has it, my love, my little darling? You see, the sky loves us; you and I are so unique. We are like children protected by God. Even the evil that comes of our crazy and fiery natures has not done us in. So, darling, think of all that you have yet to get done, and how much joy it will bring your rose, your vain rose who will say to herself: "I am the king's rose; I'm different from all other roses, because he takes care of me, and keeps me alive. He bends down to breathe in my scent . . ." And I'll tell you about all my nights filled with danger, with tears, and my nights spent waiting up hopefully for my king. And I'll bloom once again, and spread fragrance all about me so that everyone knows I am the true, the sacred rose. Your rose . . . [New York, 35 Beekman Place, October 1943]

From *Lettres du Dimanche* (*Sunday Letters*),
Plon, 2001

ANNABELLA

French actor and wife of
Tyrone Power

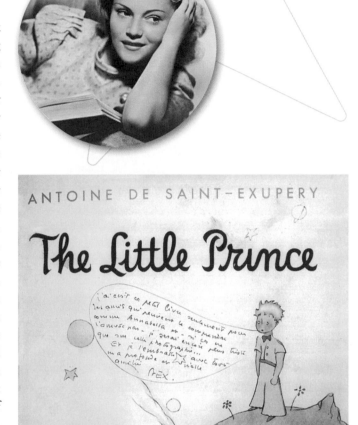

Every so often, when he went back to New York, I would get these long phone calls from him, whether I was in California or Chicago. "Listen," he'd say, "I'm going to read you the last chapter I just finished . . ." And that's how the little prince came to be a real live character in my eyes, just as real as all the actors I've acted with in my long career . . . Through this idealized character Saint-Exupéry was able to express the fact that he didn't like men as they were, that he was no great fan of modern life, of American life. Because, despite all the attention he received from Americans, he really suffered in the United States; he suffered because of the distance from France, from occupied France. He was filled with despair for his country, and he suffered for her as if from an open wound. There's no doubt that's what led him to seek refuge in the purity of the little prince; there wasn't any man to whom he could look for refuge, least of all de Gaulle.

From *Icare,* no. 84, Spring 1978

Incomplete and unique copy of *The Little Prince* given to Annabella by the author: "I wrote this little book just for some friends, like Annabella, who will understand it. If she doesn't like it, I'll be even sadder than I am in this photo . . . And I embrace her with deep appreciation of our long friendship. St Ex." Early 1943.

SILVIA HAMILTON

American journalist and
Saint-Exupéry's companion in New York

[Antoine] told me the story of the little prince even before he'd begun to write it down, back when we first met. And since he was always drawing such wonderful sketches of him, I suggested that he illustrate the book himself. [. . .] I clearly remember that he based the character of the tiger on a little pet boxer I had at the time. [. . .] He wrote a large part of the story and drew most of the illustrations at my house. At the end of each day, he'd leave me the new pages he'd written so I could "examine and comment on" them.

Then, the date of his departure drew closer, and I so wanted him to arrive safe and sound. I had a golden identity bracelet made for him. At first I didn't have all the information I needed for it, like his blood type, etc., but he eventually got it to me and I had it engraved on the bracelet and gave it to him the morning he came to say goodbye. As he was leaving, he handed me his old Zeiss Ikon camera and the French manuscript of *The Little Prince* . . .

From *Icare,* no. 84, Spring 1978

PEGGY HITCHCOCK

Wife of Curtice Hitchcock,
American publisher of *The Little Prince*

Our most relaxing moments together were spent with Bernard Lamotte in his studio. That's where we first had the pleasure of seeing the sketches of the disheveled little child and his long scarf fluttering in the wind. [Antoine] came there often . . . Genius is impressionable and often unpredictable, so it was certainly not without hesitation that Curtice finally suggested to him that he might turn this young fellow into a character, or the hero, of a children's book. One only has to look at Saint-Exupéry's correspondence to see that he was both surprised and seduced by this idea. And he dedicated himself to it (both to the story and the illustrations), at once.

On the eve of his departure he came by the house . . . If I'm not mistaken it was then that he signed several copies of *The Little Prince* and added a few sketches.

From *Icare,* no. 84, Spring 1978

The king. Sketch given to Adèle Breaux, summer of 1942.

ADÈLE BREAUX

Saint-Exupéry's English-language tutor in New York

One day, when I arrived at his place to give him his English lesson, I sensed that his study looked different . . . there was a huge pile of onionskin paper on the floor. I could make out the outlines of colored figures on some of the sheets, and I saw a box of paints, a glass of colored water, and some paintbrushes on the table to the right, by the window . . . I saw a picture of a little boy with a scarf around his neck that was blowing in the wind [. . .]. And he told me: "I had a really tough time convincing my editors that the story had to end with the death of the little prince. They told me that a children's story must never have a bad ending. I showed them that they were wrong. Children always accept anything that is natural. And death is natural . . . No child will ever feel completely devastated by the little prince's departure . . ."

From *Icare,* no. 84, Spring 1978

Jean Renoir
and Antoine de
Saint-Exupéry.

PAUL-ÉMILE VICTOR
French ethnologist and explorer

Saint-Ex had already written the text for *The Little Prince* and had drawn the first sketches of the illustrations that were to later appear in the book, but he was unsure about how to color them. He didn't like watercolors, and he felt colored pencils made the illustrations look too infantile. Then I introduced him to watercolor pencils, which I'd been using for a long time on most of my own drawings . . . we tried all kinds of things. I'm not sure which technique he ended up liking the most, but I think, based on a close analysis of the illustrations in *The Little Prince,* that he ended up using the watercolor pencils along with an ink pen for the outlines. Then he must have faded the lines by lifting some of the ink with a paintbrush.

From *Icare,* no. 84, Spring 1978

JEAN RENOIR
French film director

During the time he lived with us [in Los Angeles], he would work at night. His pockets were always stuffed with bits of paper that he'd cover with lines and lines of chicken scratch, or where he'd draw outlines of pictures you'd then see in *The Little Prince.* And since he was about the only person who could decipher his own handwriting, at night he'd take out the pieces of paper and read them out loud into the Dictaphone.

From *Icare,* no. 84, Spring 1978

NELLY DE VOGÜÉ
Saint-Exupéry's friend and confidante
(pen name Pierre Chevrier)

He's sad and he's lonely, and he's always distracting himself by drawing little princes with startled or disappointed faces on scraps of paper.

"Your little fellow ought to talk," a friend once told him, "he should tell us what he's thinking."

"Oh, the things he thinks about! . . ." was his answer.

"Even the strongest among us, in a moment of exhaustion, will look for the safety of a shoulder to rest his head on."

"That would be a bit sad," Saint-Exupéry muttered, as if he were talking about himself [. . .].

Is the only way he can bare his soul to us, then, through the innocent voice of a child? Perhaps, but he certainly wouldn't admit to it. And if someone who knows him well should recognize the man in the revelations of the child, and think to call him out on it, Saint-Exupéry would most certainly answer, "Yes, you've guessed correctly, but you mustn't tell anyone."

Note from Pierre Chevrier [Nelly de Vogüé],
Antoine de Saint-Exupéry, Gallimard, 1949

PIERRE LAZAREFF
French journalist and newspaper publisher

Often Saint-Ex would call me during the night and say, "I just wrote five more pages; I'm going to read them to you." [. . .] "Do you like them?" Then, when he'd finished reading them, he would reread the ending, sobbing, as if he'd foreseen his own death that would so resemble that of the little prince.

DENIS DE ROUGEMONT
Swiss writer and friend of the Saint-Exupérys

Bevin House: I'm with the Saint-Exes at their new country house, two hours from New York City. This is how I spend my thirty-six hours of leave every week. It was Consuelo who found the house. In fact, you'd think she'd designed it herself, it's so immense. It sits on a promontory surrounded by trees disheveled from all the storms. But the house itself is protected on three sides by a series of winding waterways that encroach gently upon the forested landscape and small tropic-like islands.

The first time he set foot in the place, Tonio quipped: "All I wanted was a shack and what I got is the Palace of Versailles!" But now you couldn't get him to leave if you tried! He's started working again on a children's book that he's illustrating with his own watercolors. He's like a bald giant with round, eagle-like eyes, and yet he handles tiny, child-sized paintbrushes with surgical precision. And when he's working and concentrating really hard to avoid making a mistake he grimaces. I pose as the little prince for him, lying on my stomach with my legs up in the air, and Tonio laughs like a madman: "One day, you'll be pointing this picture out to someone and you'll be able to say—'That's me!'" In the evening he reads us excerpts from an enormous book ("I'm going to read you my posthumous work"), the one I think is his best [*The Wisdom of the Sands*]. Late at night, I finally go to my room exhausted (I have to be in the city by 9:00 the next morning), but he comes in again, to smoke cigarettes and talk about world events. His energy is tireless. I get the impression his brain just can't shut down anymore . . .

From *Journal d'une Époque (Journal of an Epoch), 1926–1946*, Gallimard, 1968

The little prince on the wall; the little prince lying down. Sketches, summer of 1942.

ANDRÉ MAUROIS
French author and
member of the French Academy

It's been only four years since he wrote *The Little Prince* in Bevin House, an ocean-side home close to New York City. The Saint-Exupérys had a way of finding these strange, superhuman places to live in that were always way too big for them. It's as if they needed extra rooms to house ghosts. This particular house was in Eatons Neck, in Northport (Asharoken, Long Island), in a deserted spot surrounded by waterways and marshes. When I visited there, the trees were ablaze with the fiery colors of a New England autumn. I had arrived with Denis de Rougemont [October 1942], and we'd spent the afternoon listening to Saint-Ex's amazing stories. He was such a prodigious raconteur; he could have us traversing Indochina and the suburbs of Paris, the Sahara Desert and the high reaches of Chile all in one afternoon.

After dinner Saint-Ex would play chess and perform the cleverest card tricks I've ever seen. The pleasure this gave him was both magical and poetic. Afterwards, at midnight, he'd go into his study and stay there working on the story and illustrations of *The Little Prince* whose hero, on his tiny planet, was really a projection of his own self. Then, in the middle of the night, he'd come call us into his study to show us a drawing he was particularly pleased with. I suppose imposing and lavishing one's life on others is a mark of genius.

From *Les Nouvelles littéraires,* November 7, 1946

Drawings for Max Gelée, May 1943: "This is one of today's student pilots. When one studies aviation one learns all about slowness . . .";"The wings won't suffice for lift-off."

MAX GELÉE

French general and commander of Air Force Squadron 2/33 (May 1943)

No sooner had he gotten in touch with us, than Saint-Exupéry took me aside and said: "Quick, come look what I've done with my butterfly catcher! . . ."

Then, with infinite precaution, he pulled out the only French copy he had of *The Little Prince*—without once letting it out of his hands, of course. You wouldn't even dream of asking to hold it yourself.

He explained it like this:

> You know, I put my heart and soul into this. I've had to redo each drawing several times, because the publisher was never satisfied. Look, here's the one I struggled over the most: I wanted to draw a planet with three enormous trees, but I barely managed to draw one tree. And once I'd managed that one I couldn't drum up the courage to draw the other two. So, in the end I decided to rotate the picture, twice, each time by 120 degrees, and to copy the first tree exactly as it was in the other two places. That's how I managed to get the drawing of the planet with the three baobabs to be just how I wanted it . . .

There's no greater proof of the state of distress he was in during that eight-month period (between his two missions flying as part of Reconnaissance Group II/33) than in those drawings. The subject was always the same: the butterfly catcher, in some form or another. But, whatever his situation, he had one trait that was always the same: he was always miserable, terribly sad . . . Dressed as a gardener, this particular little prince was contemplating a winged snail and saying to him: "Your wings won't be enough for lift-off."

From *Icare,* no. 96, Spring 1981

JULES ROY
French author and member
of the British Royal Air Force

A few days later, as I was coming down from the hotel terrace [. . .] I found him there, waiting for me, his nose held up in the air. And suddenly it occurred to me that I looked like the lamplighter he'd drawn for the edition of *The Little Prince* he'd brought back with him from New York. We went back to his room and he collapsed onto the bed, his owl-like eyes staring up at the ceiling. He was smoking and inhaling intensely and, after a long silence, he poured out all his anguish. He didn't want to admit how desperate he was, but he suffered flesh and soul for France's plight. He was burning with fever from his inability to bring her immediate succor as she lay there suffocating. France, to him, was the quintessential embodiment of all that a motherland could be, and he saw her oppression as the oppression of all humanity.

From that moment on I had the impression that [his] *Letter to a Hostage,* of which I'd only read a few sections, and *The Little Prince,* which I'd just read in its entirety, must have been conceived within the grip of this deep despair.

From *Passion de Saint-Exupéry,* Gallimard, 1951

PIERRE GUILLAIN DE BÉNOUVILLE
French author and political figure

In the days that followed I saw as much of Saint-Exupéry as possible. Sometimes he'd come to our house; other times we'd go visit him at his apartment. Walking down the hallway we'd see that the floor of his bedroom was strewn with papers. He'd take us to the sitting room and fix us a drink. He'd hand us some books and then he'd hand us *The Little Prince;* it was clear that he saw it as his autobiography. He'd hand it to us smiling, as if he'd just handed us a photo of himself.

From *Confluences,* no. 12, 1947

GEORGES PÉLISSIER
Surgeon in Algiers and
friend of Saint-Exupéry

Antoine found only one fault with *The Little Prince* (for which he had a singular predilection): it included "just a few too many planets." By this he meant that he would have willingly left out some of the little prince's interplanetary voyages, although I'm sure he wouldn't have taken out the part about the lamplighter.

From *Les Cinq Visages de Saint-Exupéry* (*The Five Faces of Saint-Exupéry*), Flammarion, 1951

With John Phillips in Alghero, Sardinia, May 1944.

JOHN PHILLIPS
American photojournalist

I'd often seen this little prince raise his head from Saint-Exupéry's papers before, but I'd never dared ask him how such a little elf of a character could have so imposed himself on him. He explained to me that one day, as he sat staring at a blank sheet of paper, the little fellow had just suddenly appeared there. "Who are you?" Saint-Ex had asked him. "I'm the little prince," he'd answered. And while Saint-Ex had no shortage of people to play games with (he liked Scrabble), there the little fellow was, always at his side.

From *Au Revoir, Saint-Ex,* Gallimard, 1994

ANNE MORROW LINDBERGH
Author, aviator, and wife of Charles Lindbergh

St.-Ex.'s fairy story [*The Little Prince*] comes and I read it with impatience at one sitting. But it is so terribly sad—sadder than the war book really. In spite of the fact that it is simply a very lightly painted, charming fable—fairy story for children. (No, not for children at all. He does not know what a child is. His little prince is a saint, not a child. He is an adult with the heart of a child. He is the really "pure in heart," like Dostoevsky's *Idiot.* But he is not a child. He has not "the hard heart of a child." He is more like a woman who has never grown up.) But the sadness is not the sadness of war or tragedy. It is personal sadness—eternal sadness, eternal hunger, eternal searching. It is unbearably "nostalgique," but a nostalgia for "the light that never was, on sea or land."

One wants to comfort him. (I feel he must have been miserable and sick and lonely whcn he wrote it.) And knows it is not possible.

There are beautiful things in it, too, all vulnerability, all tenderness, all hurt. And some answers.

But no, he has not the answers for personal life. He has not found them. And I am afraid he never will. He will throw himself into self-sacrifice—war and death.

Thinking that is the answer, and it is not.

Journal entry, March 29, 1943, from *Écrits de Guerre* (*Wartime Writings*), *1939–1944,* Gallimard, 1982

The author's mother, Marie de Saint-Exupéry, in the garden at Saint-Maurice-de-Rémens, about 1910.

SIMONE DE SAINT-EXUPÉRY
Archivist, paleographer, and older sister of Antoine de Saint-Exupéry

I was so touched when, returning from Indochina in 1946, I first became acquainted with this little book in which the characters I remembered from the letters he wrote me as a child reappeared in fresh clothes. I had been living in the Far East for seven years, and it was there that I first heard of his disappearance . . .

Despite the kindness of Americans and the immense esteem the publication of *Flight to Arras* had earned him, his years in the States marked him terribly. He suffered there, not only because of the occupation of his country, or because news of his loved ones was difficult to come by, but also because of the state of mind many of his fellow Frenchmen were in there in the States. And he was haunted by the childhood years he spent with his brother and sisters in Saint-Maurice-de-Rémens, by the games they played in the flower-filled garden and the shady copse. *The Little Prince* was an escape, a gathering together of all that had been joyful, first in the life of a child with golden locks, and then in the life of a rowdy schoolboy who lived on his own enchanted planet, the planet of childhood. In a way, the little fellow was [Saint-Ex's] twin come to stand beside the aviator who'd fallen victim to the risks of his occupation, the crashes in the desert, the thirst, the anguish and the solitude one feels among the sands where yellow snakes slither about in waiting. If he poured his whole heart into the illustrations he made for *The Little Prince,* it is because they were a way for him to express his innermost feelings, those that his modesty as a writer would prevent him from revealing in words. He'd written to his mother: "It's difficult to talk about one's innermost feelings . . . it feels so pretentious." The nostalgia he felt for the past, flowers, family pets he'd tamed, the magical poetry he harbored within and which he found difficult to express in any way other than through fairy tales, were all there, hidden in his drawings.

Portrait of Simone de Saint-Exupéry by her brother Antoine. Undated.

From *Musées et collections publiques de France et de l'Union française,* no. 17, 1958

LÉON WERTH

French art critic and essayist; dedicatee of *The Little Prince*

Saint-Exupéry had a magic touch when it came to people and places. He connected with them naturally and effortlessly. For not only did he have the ability to charm children, but he could also persuade grown-ups they themselves were as real as the characters in a fairy tale. He'd never chased his own childhood out of his system. Grown-ups only understand their fellow man vaguely, through bits and pieces of information: their understanding of him is poor at best. Children, on the other hand, see their fellow man with absolute clarity. His true nature is as clear to them as is that of an Ogre, or Sleeping Beauty. In the world of children everything is black and white. And Saint-Exupéry's gift lay in his ability to offer this same level of clarity to grown-ups so that anyone who was around him would come away knowing himself better than he did before, as if he were Tom Thumb himself.

From *Saint-Exupéry tel que Je l'Ai Connu (The Saint-Exupéry I Knew)*, Viviane Hamy, 1994

Drawing for Léon Werth. "My soul, on rainy days. A."

"*This grown-up is the best friend I have in the world.*"

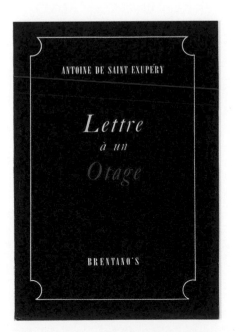

First American edition of *Letter to a Hostage*, June 1943. The text had been intended as the preface for *33 Days*, Léon Werth's memoir of his June 1940 escape from Paris.

"A CRUMBLING OLD WALL LADEN IN IVY"

We are both sprung from the same childhood. Whenever I think back on it, there rises up before my mind the vision of that old, crumbling, ivy-covered wall. We were bold children. "What are you scared of? Push open the door."

Yes, an old, crumbling, ivy-covered wall. Dried up, scorched, and seared with sunlight, hardened to a crisp in the oven of slow time. Through the leaves the lizards rustled, those "snakes" as we called them, for already our spirits were captivated by the image of flight, of death. On this side each stone was warm, brooded over by the sun overhead like an egg in its roost. Each twig was stripped of all mystery by the sun. On this side of the wall summer, in all its plentitude, reigned over the countryside. We could see the church steeple, hear a thresher working. The blue of the sky filled every nook and cranny. The peasants were scything their wheat fields, the curé spraying his vines; the grown-ups in the salon were playing bridge. We had a name for those who, for sixty years or more and from birth to death, had worked this soil, had taken this sun, these wheat fields, this property into custody: these living generations we called "The Watch." For we liked to think of ourselves as a sea-girt isle, hemmed in between two perilous oceans, the past and the future.

"Turn the key . . ."

We children were forbidden to open the little green door, whose paint had faded like a timbered hull, or to touch the massive lock, rusted by the years like an old sea anchor . . .

"Let's sit down . . ."

Here not a sound would reach us. We drank in the freshness of the smell, the coolness of the damp that revived our bodies. We were lost, on the very confines of the world, for already we knew that to travel is above all to change one's skin.

"Here everything is backwards . . ."

From *Southern Mail*, 1929

Left to right:
Marie-Madeleine,
Gabrielle,
François, Antoine,
and Simone de
Saint-Exupéry,
about 1907.

"WE . . . SAW A STAR, ONE SOLITARY STAR, FALL ON US"

Escape, that was the thing! When we were ten we found refuge in the attic's timber-work among the dead birds, old bursting trunks, amazing garments: it was a bit like being in the wings of the stage of life. And we were sure there was a treasure hidden there; there's always a secret treasure in old houses, just like in fairy tales: sapphires, opals, and diamonds. The treasure here shone feebly. Surely, it was the raison d'être of each wall, each beam. And the huge beams defended the house against we-knew-not-what. But yes, actually, we did—it was against time. For time was the archenemy and it was upon us. We kept it at bay with traditions, the cult of the past, and the huge beams. But we knew that this house was launched like a ship. We who visited its holds and bulkheads knew just where she was leaking. We knew the holes in the roof through which the little birds slipped in to die. We knew each crack in the timbering. Meanwhile, downstairs in the drawing rooms, the guests conversed and the pretty ladies danced. What a deceptive sense of security they had! No doubt they were being offered liqueurs by white-gloved butlers in black coats. How fleeting! While we, up there, watched the blue night filter through the crannies in the roof, and saw a star, one solitary star, fall on us through a tiny hole. Imagine! It was decanted just for us from the vast expanse of the heavens. But it was the star that brings malaise. So we hastily turned away, fearful of the kiss of death.

Often we would jump with fright over the hidden ways of things. The beams would creak, as though split by the treasure, and at each sound we would probe the wood. It was like a giant peapod getting ready to yield its grain. It was all a time worn husk beneath which, we were certain, something else lay hidden—be it no more than that star, that small hard diamond. One day we would sally forth—northwards, southwards, or into ourselves—in quest of it. Ah yes, escape!

From *Southern Mail,* 1929

* *

∗ ∗

"EACH STAR SHOWS A TRUE DIRECTION"

I spent three years living in the Sahara. Like many others I mused over its magic. Anyone who has lived in the Sahara, where solitude and barrenness seem all enveloping, thereafter cherishes these years as the most worthwhile he has ever known. [. . .]

True, in the Sahara the sand or, more precisely, stony expanses (dunes being rare) stretch away as far as the eye can see. There one is permanently plunged into conditions that appear to be conducive to boredom. And yet invisible gods endow the desert with any number of trails, slopes, signs, a secret and living framework, so that there is no uniformity left. Everything finds its place. Even one silence differs from another. [. . .]

Everything is polarized. Each star shows a true direction. They are all stars of Bethlehem—each serves its own god. This one points to a far-off well that is difficult to reach, and the distance between you and the well is as heavy as a rampart. That one points to a dried-up well. The star itself seems dried-up. The distance between you and the dried-up well seems flat. Another star guides you to an unknown oasis that the nomads sing of, which a revolt prevents you from visiting. The sand that separates you from the oasis is a fairy tale lawn. [. . .]

Finally, the Earth's poles, as unreal as they might seem, pull at this desert from a great distance: it becomes a childhood home vividly remembered, a friend one knows nothing of, except that he exists.

From *Letter to a Hostage,* 1943

∗ ∗

LETTER TO MADAME DE ROSE

Dear Yvonne,

I have to thank you for many things—I don't know what they are (the things that count are invisible), but I'm right no doubt, since I feel like thanking you. That's not exactly it—one doesn't thank a garden. I've always divided human beings into two categories: those who resemble a courtyard and suffocate you between their walls—whom you are forced to speak to in order to make a noise because silence is painful in a courtyard.

Then there are those who resemble a garden, where you can walk, and be silent, and breathe. One feels at ease and experiences pleasant surprises. There is nothing to look for: a butterfly, a scarab, a glowworm, appear. One knows nothing of the life habits of a glowworm. One muses. The scarab seems to know where it's going. It's in a great hurry. That is surprising. Then when the butterfly settles on a large flower, one says to oneself: *"It's as if it landed on the terrace of one of the hanging gardens of Babylon, swaying gently to and fro."* Then one is silent because of three or four stars.

In fact, I don't thank you at all—you are yourself and I feel like taking a stroll with you.

There are also people who resemble main roads and people who resemble country paths. The former bore me with their tarmac and their milestones. They lead somewhere definite—toward a profit or an ambition. Along the country paths there are nut trees instead of milestones, and one strolls along in order to crunch nuts—for no other reason. There is no set purpose, no ulterior motive. One walks along in order to take a stroll. But nothing is to be got out of milestones.

May 1944

Drawings and Watercolors

Antoine de Saint-Exupéry

Drawings, late 1930s and early 1940s.

✦
✦
✦
✦
✦
✦

"What a lovely thing
the side of a hill is."

Drawings, late 1930s.

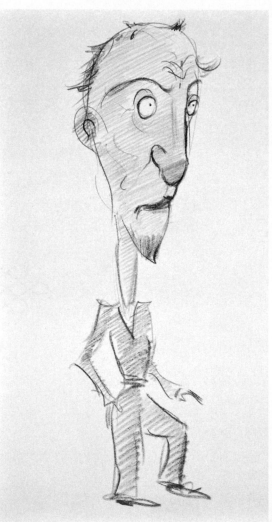

*
*
*
*
*

"Grown-ups are so strange."

Drawing for Nelly de Vogüé.

"Ah! Jean-Gérard Fleury, if this pig catches me, I'll never see you again. St-Ex." A Block 174 (French plane) being chased by a Messerschmitt 109 (German plane).

A little prince with wings

Letter to Léon Werth, spring of 1939.

The winged little prince (below) has its roots in these aerial battle images from the May–June 1940 French aerial offensive, in which Saint-Exupéry took part as a pilot.

"All the stars are blossoming."

Star tree, from the margin of a manuscript page.

Drawing from the 1930s kept by Nelly de Vogüé.

"And are there no people on Earth?"

Two enigmatic allegories: "What's the point?" and "All things considered, she is bored." Drawings kept by Nelly de Vogüé.

146

Sketch for the illustration in Chapter XVII (page 130).

Sources of inspiration for Antoine de Saint-Exupéry's small animals: "The butterfly catcher" (sketch for *The Little Prince,* summer of 1942); figure with a small dog (late 1930s); the little prince and the snail (sketch from the summer of 1942); Youki, the dog; sketches for the little prince's tiger (summer of 1942).

Bestiary

KAUMAIRE
COMER

First sketches

Debout sur la tour la plus haute, [illegible], comme un ramoneur [illegible], sur [illegible] la nuit, je contemplais mon Empire [illegible]

[illegible]

[illegible]

[illegible] décombres [illegible]

[illegible]

[illegible]

[illegible]

[illegible]

[illegible]

[illegible]

[illegible]

[illegible] nuit.

[illegible]

[illegible] antiques [illegible]

[illegible]

[illegible]

Images of the bond

The little prince with a balloon; the little prince
with the fox. Two pencil drawings, 1942–43.

Two drawings to accompany the typewritten
manuscript of *The Little Prince* given as a gift
to the pianist Nadia Boulanger, 1942.

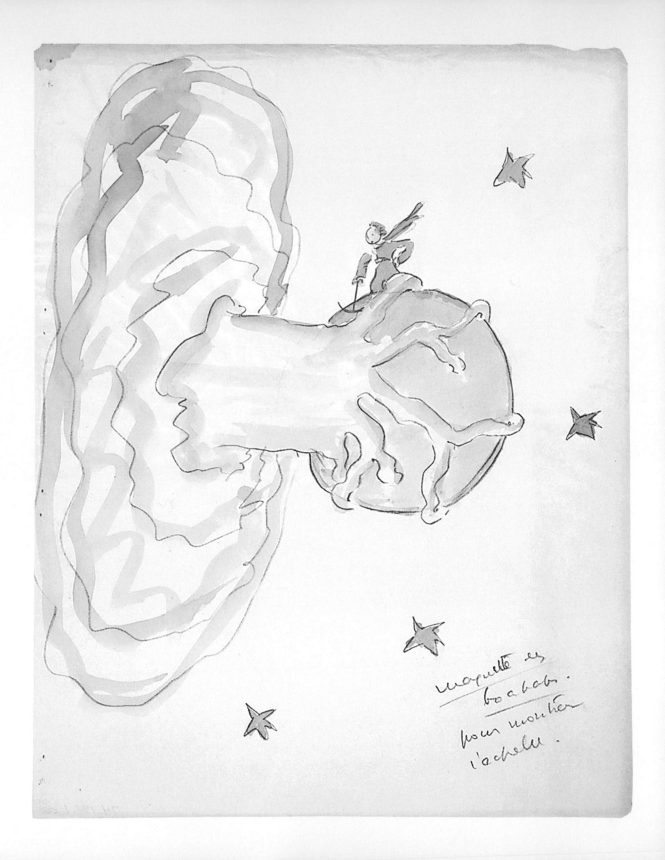

Sketches for Lewis Galantière

"Model of the baobabs to show the scale" and "It isn't a drawing; it's a mock-up to show the scale." Two drawings entrusted to his translator, Lewis Galantière, by Antoine de Saint-Exupéry, January 1943 (see page 15).

Drawings for Silvia Hamilton

Sketches: the scene where the little prince talks with the snake while sitting on the old stone wall (Chapter XXVI, page 155); the king (Chapter X, page 108).

The herd of elephants (Chapter V, page 94); the hunter (Chapter XXI, page 139): original watercolors for the 1943 printing of *The Little Prince.*

"The little prince has died. Or, rather, he has become completely disillusioned."

"I even sent you a few lines but you haven't acknowledged them . . . That's why, young invisible lady, I've invented this little girl here who is going to become my friend, just like the little prince was, and I will tell you her story. [. . .] She's very sad, because she doesn't know yet that I'm her great friend." *Letters to a Stranger*, Algeria, 1943–44.

The metamorphosis of the little prince, as seen on a handwritten page entrusted by the author to Hedda Sterne, 1942 or 1943.

Création cruauté spasme, recherche sans savoir possible. Poète
extrêmement mais contracté en soi avec colère. Tue ce qui le peine ne
s'oppose à lui. Rompu net. Sans orgueil en temps croquées (en soi
mais S'orgueil total ordure ni ni dehors. Pas toile les majorité des
femmes sans la discussion. Femmes avec sa besogne après — mais il ne
s'agit jamais d'un truc pensez.si car il ne peut rien ni ni crié
douce. ni colorié. Plutôt à manque. Aucun effort social. Que
l'on ne morde sur lui. Le suicideraa.

Letters to a Stranger, 1943–44

"She's never there when I call her . . . She never goes home at night . . . She doesn't call . . . I'm burning with desire for her! [Burn mark on the sheet of paper] And it's not very nice of her not to call me or come see me, because I don't forget people that easily and I really want . . . [The bird:] So, is your letter finished or not? Because I need to deliver it! . . . [The little prince:] Sorry, I was writing to a friend who's completely forgotten about me." *Letters to a Stranger,* Algeria, 1943–44.

In order to make his escape, I believe he took advantage
of a migration of wild birds.

The Little Prince

WRITTEN AND ILLUSTRATED BY

ANTOINE DE SAINT-EXUPÉRY

TRANSLATED FROM THE FRENCH BY RICHARD HOWARD

HOUGHTON MIFFLIN HARCOURT

Boston   New York

TO LEON WERTH

I ask children to forgive me for dedicating this book to a grown-up. I have a serious excuse: this grown-up is the best friend I have in the world. I have another excuse: this grown-up can understand everything, even books for children. I have a third excuse: he lives in France where he is hungry and cold. He needs to be comforted. If all these excuses are not enough, then I want to dedicate this book to the child whom this grown-up once was. All grown-ups were children first. (But few of them remember it.) So I correct my dedication:

TO LEON WERTH
WHEN HE WAS A LITTLE BOY

I

Once when i was six I saw a magnificent picture in a book about the jungle, called *True Stories*. It showed a boa constrictor swallowing a wild beast. Here is a copy of the picture.

In the book it said: "Boa constrictors swallow their prey whole, without chewing. Afterward they are no longer able to move, and they sleep during the six months of their digestion."

In those days I thought a lot about jungle adventures, and eventually managed to make my first drawing, using a colored pencil. My drawing Number One looked like this:

I showed the grown-ups my masterpiece, and I asked them if my drawing scared them.

They answered, "Why be scared of a hat?"

My drawing was not a picture of a hat. It was a picture of a boa constrictor digesting an elephant. Then I drew the inside of the boa constrictor, so the grown-ups could understand. They always need explanations. My drawing Number Two looked like this:

The grown-ups advised me to put away my drawings of boa constrictors, outside or inside, and apply myself instead to geography, history, arithmetic, and grammar. That is why I abandoned, at the age of six, a magnificent career as an artist. I had been discouraged by the failure of my drawing Number One and of my drawing Number Two. Grown-ups never understand anything by themselves, and it is exhausting for children to have to provide explanations over and over again.

So then I had to choose another career, and I learned to pilot airplanes. I have flown almost everywhere in the world. And, as a matter of fact, geography has been a big help to me. I could tell China from Arizona at first glance, which is very useful if you get lost during the night.

So I have had, in the course of my life, lots of encounters with lots of serious people. I have spent lots of time with grown-ups. I have seen them at close range . . . which hasn't much improved my opinion of them.

Whenever I encountered a grown-up who seemed to me at all enlightened, I would experiment on him with my drawing Number One, which I have always kept. I wanted to see if he really understood anything. But he would always answer, "That's a hat." Then I wouldn't talk about boa constrictors or jungles or stars. I would put myself on his level and talk about bridge and golf and politics and neckties. And my grown-up was glad to know such a reasonable person.

II

SO I LIVED all alone, without anyone I could really talk to, until I had to make a crash landing in the Sahara Desert six years ago. Something in my plane's engine had broken, and since I had neither a mechanic nor passengers in the plane with me, I was preparing to undertake the difficult repair job by myself. For me it was a matter of life or death: I had only enough drinking water for eight days.

The first night, then, I went to sleep on the sand a thousand miles from any inhabited country. I was more isolated than a man shipwrecked on a raft in the middle of the ocean. So you can imagine my surprise when I was awakened at daybreak by a funny little voice saying, "Please . . . draw me a sheep . . ."

"What?"

"Draw me a sheep . . ."

I leaped up as if I had been struck by lightning. I rubbed my eyes hard. I stared. And I saw an extraordinary little fellow staring back at me very seriously. Here is the best portrait I managed to make of him, later on. But of course my drawing is much less attractive than my model. This is not my fault. My career as a painter was discouraged at the age of six by the grown-ups, and I had never learned to draw anything except boa constrictors, outside and inside.

So I stared wide-eyed at this apparition. Don't forget that I was a thousand miles from any inhabited territory. Yet this little fellow seemed to be neither lost nor dying of exhaustion, hunger, or thirst; nor did he seem scared to death. There was nothing in his appearance that suggested a child lost in the middle of the desert a thousand miles from any inhabited territory. When I finally managed to speak, I asked him, "But . . . what are you doing here?"

And then he repeated, very slowly and very seriously, "Please . . . draw me a sheep . . ."

In the face of an overpowering mystery, you don't dare disobey. Absurd as it seemed, a thousand miles from all inhabited regions and in danger of death, I took a scrap of paper and a pen out of my pocket. But then I remembered that I had mostly studied geography, history, arithmetic, and grammar, and I told the little fellow (rather crossly) that I didn't know how to draw.

He replied, "That doesn't matter. Draw me a sheep."

Since I had never drawn a sheep, I made him one of the

Here is the best portrait I managed to make of him, later on.

only two drawings I knew how to make—the one of the boa constrictor from outside. And I was astounded to hear the little fellow answer:

"No! No! I don't want an elephant inside a boa constrictor. A boa constrictor is very dangerous, and an elephant would get in the way. Where I live, everything is very small. I need a sheep. Draw me a sheep."

So then I made a drawing.

He looked at it carefully, and then said, "No. This one is already quite sick. Make another."

I made another drawing. My friend gave me a kind, indulgent smile:

"You can see for yourself . . . that's not a sheep, it's a ram. It has horns . . ."

So I made my third drawing, but it was rejected, like the others:

"This one's too old. I want a sheep that will live a long time."

So then, impatiently, since I was in a hurry to start work on my engine, I scribbled this drawing, and added, "This is just the crate. The sheep you want is inside."

But I was amazed to see my young critic's face light up. "That's just the kind I wanted! Do you think this sheep will need a lot of grass?"

"Why?"

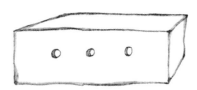

"Because where I live, everything is very small . . ."

"There's sure to be enough. I've given you a very small sheep."

He bent over the drawing. "Not so small as all that . . . Look! He's gone to sleep . . ."

And that's how I made the acquaintance of the little prince.

III

IT TOOK ME a long time to understand where he came from. The little prince, who asked me so many questions, never seemed to hear the ones I asked him. It was things he said quite at random that, bit by bit, explained everything. For instance, when he first caught sight of my airplane (I won't draw my airplane; that would be much too complicated for me) he asked:

"What's that thing over there?"

"It's not a thing. It flies. It's an airplane. My airplane."

And I was proud to tell him I could fly. Then he exclaimed:

"What! You fell out of the sky?"

"Yes," I said modestly.

"Oh! That's funny . . ." And the little prince broke into a lovely peal of laughter, which annoyed me a good deal. I like my misfortunes to be taken seriously. Then he added, "So you fell out of the sky, too. What planet are you from?"

That was when I had the first clue to the mystery of his presence, and I questioned him sharply. "Do you come from another planet?"

But he made no answer. He shook his head a little, still staring at my airplane. "Of course, *that* couldn't have brought you from very far . . ." And he fell into a reverie that lasted a long while. Then, taking my sheep out of his pocket, he plunged into contemplation of his treasure.

You can imagine how intrigued I was by this hint about "other planets." I tried to learn more: "Where do you come from, little fellow? Where is this 'where I live' of yours? Where will you be taking my sheep?"

After a thoughtful silence he answered, "The good thing about the crate you've given me is that he can use it for a house after dark."

"Of course. And if you're good, I'll give you a rope to tie him up during the day. And a stake to tie him to."

This proposition seemed to shock the little prince.

"Tie him up! What a funny idea!"

"But if you don't tie him up, he'll wander off somewhere and get lost."

My friend burst out laughing again. "Where could he go?"

"Anywhere. Straight ahead . . ."

Then the little prince remarked quite seriously, "Even if he did, everything's so small where I live!" And he added, perhaps a little sadly, "Straight ahead, you can't go very far."

IV

THAT WAS HOW I had learned a second very important thing, which was that the planet he came from was hardly bigger than a house!

That couldn't surprise me much. I knew very well that except for the huge planets like Earth, Jupiter, Mars, and Venus, which have been given names, there are hundreds of others that are sometimes so small that it's very difficult to see them through a telescope. When an astronomer discovers one of them, he gives it a number instead of a name. For instance, he would call it "Asteroid 325."

I have serious reasons to believe that the planet the little prince came from is Asteroid B-612. This asteroid has been sighted only once by telescope, in 1909 by a Turkish astronomer, who had then made a formal demonstration of his discovery at an International Astronomical Congress. But no one had believed him on account of the way he was dressed. Grown-ups are like that.

Fortunately for the reputation of Asteroid B-612, a Turkish dictator ordered his people, on pain of death, to wear European clothes. The astronomer repeated his

demonstration in 1920, wearing a very elegant suit. And this time everyone believed him.

If I've told you these details about Asteroid B-612 and if I've given you its number, it is on account of the grown-ups. Grown-ups like numbers. When you tell them about a new friend, they never ask questions about what really matters. They never ask: "What does his voice sound like?" "What games does he like best?" "Does he collect butter-flies?" They ask: "How old is he?" "How many brothers does he have?" "How much does he weigh?" "How much money does his father make?" Only then do they think they know him. If you tell grown-ups, "I saw a beauti-ful red brick house, with geraniums at the windows and doves on the roof . . . ," they won't be able to imagine such a house. You have to tell them, "I saw a house worth a hundred thousand francs." Then they ex-claim, "What a pretty house!"

The Little Prince on Asteroid B-612

So if you tell them: "The proof of the little prince's existence is that he was delightful, that he laughed, and that he wanted a sheep. When someone wants a sheep, that proves he exists," they shrug their shoulders and treat you like a child! But if you tell them, "The planet he came from is Asteroid B-612," then they'll be convinced, and they won't bother you with their questions. That's the way they are. You must not hold it against them. Children should be very understanding of grown-ups.

But, of course, those of us who understand life couldn't care less about numbers! I should have liked to begin this story like a fairy tale. I should have liked to say:

"Once upon a time there was a little prince who lived on a planet hardly any bigger than he was, and who needed a friend . . ." For those who understand life, that would sound much truer.

The fact is, I don't want my book to be taken lightly. Telling these memories is so painful for me. It's already been six years since my friend went away, taking his sheep with him. If I try to describe him here, it's so I won't forget him. It's sad to forget a friend. Not everyone has had a friend. And I might become like the grown-ups who are no longer interested in anything but numbers. Which is still another reason why I've bought a box of paints and some pencils. It's hard to go back to drawing, at my age, when you've never made any attempts since the one of a boa from inside and the one of a boa from outside, at the age of six! I'll certainly try to make my portraits as true to life as possible. But I'm not entirely sure of succeeding. One drawing works, and the next no longer bears any resemblance. And I'm a little off on his height, too. In this one the little prince is too tall. And here he's too short. And I'm uncertain about the color of his suit. So I grope in one direction and another, as best I can. In the end, I'm sure to get certain more important details all wrong. But here you'll have to forgive me. My friend never explained anything. Perhaps he thought I was like himself. But I, unfortunately, cannot see a sheep through the sides of a crate. I may be a little like the grown-ups. I must have grown old.

V

EVERY DAY I'D LEARN something about the little prince's planet, about his departure, about his journey. It would come quite gradually, in the course of his remarks. This was how I learned, on the third day, about the drama of the baobabs.

This time, too, I had the sheep to thank, for suddenly the little prince asked me a question, as if overcome by a grave doubt.

"Isn't it true that sheep eat bushes?"

"Yes, that's right."

"Ah! I'm glad."

I didn't understand why it was so important that sheep should eat bushes. But the little prince added:

"And therefore they eat baobabs, too?"

I pointed out to the little prince that baobabs are not bushes but trees as tall as churches, and that even if he took a whole herd of elephants back to his planet, that herd couldn't finish off a single baobab.

The idea of the herd of elephants made the little prince laugh.

"We'd have to pile them on top of one another."

But he observed perceptively:

"Before they grow big, baobabs start out by being little."

"True enough! But why do you want your sheep to eat little baobabs?"

He answered, "Oh, come on! You know!" as if we were talking about something quite obvious. And I was forced to make a great mental effort to understand this problem all by myself.

And, in fact, on the little prince's planet there were—as on all planets—good plants and bad plants. The good plants come from good seeds, and the bad plants from bad seeds. But the seeds are invisible. They sleep in the secrecy of the ground until one of them decides to wake up. Then it stretches and begins to sprout, quite timidly at first, a charming, harmless little twig reaching toward the sun. If it's a radish seed, or a rosebush seed, you can let it sprout all it likes. But if it's the seed of a bad plant,

you must pull the plant up right away, as soon
as you can recognize it. As it happens, there were
terrible seeds on the little prince's planet . . . baobab
seeds. The planet's soil was infested with them. Now
if you attend to a baobab too late, you can never get
rid of it again. It overgrows the whole planet. Its roots
pierce right through. And if the planet is too small, and
if there are too many baobabs, they make it burst into
pieces.

"It's a question of discipline," the little prince told
me later on. "When you've finished washing and dressing
each morning, you must tend your planet. You must be
sure you pull up the baobabs regularly, as soon as you can
tell them apart from the rosebushes, which they closely
resemble when they're very young. It's very tedious work,
but very easy."

And one day he advised me to do my best to make a beautiful drawing, for the edification of the children where I live. "If they travel someday," he told me, "it could be useful to them. Sometimes there's no harm in postponing your work until later. But with baobabs, it's always a catastrophe. I knew one planet that was inhabited by a lazy man. He had neglected three bushes . . ."

So, following the little prince's instructions, I have drawn that planet. I don't much like assuming the tone of a moralist. But the danger of baobabs is so little recognized, and the risks run by anyone who might get lost on an asteroid are so considerable, that for once I am making an exception to my habitual reserve. I say, "Children, watch out for baobabs!" It's to warn my friends of a danger of which they, like myself, have long been unaware that I worked so hard on this drawing. The lesson I'm teaching is worth the trouble. You may be asking, "Why are there no other drawings in this book as big as the drawing of the baobabs?" There's a simple answer: I tried but I couldn't manage it. When I drew the baobabs, I was inspired by a sense of urgency.

VI

O LITTLE PRINCE! Gradually, this was how I came to understand your sad little life. For a long time your only entertainment was the pleasure of sunsets. I learned this new detail on the morning of the fourth day, when you told me:

The Baobabs

"I really like sunsets.
Let's go look at one now . . ."
"But we have to wait . . ."
"What for?"
"For the sun to set."
At first you seemed quite surprised, and then you
laughed at yourself. And you said to me, "I think I'm still
at home!"
Indeed. When it's noon in the United States, the sun,
as everyone knows, is setting over France. If you could fly
to France in one minute, you could watch the sunset.
Unfortunately France is much too far. But on your
tiny planet, all you had to do was move your
chair a few feet. And you would watch the
twilight whenever you wanted to. . . .

"One day I saw the sun set forty-four times!" And a little later you added, "You know, when you're feeling very sad, sunsets are wonderful . . ."

"On the day of the forty-four times, were you feeling very sad?"

But the little prince didn't answer.

VII

ON THE FIFTH DAY, thanks again to the sheep, another secret of the little prince's life was revealed to me. Abruptly, with no preamble, he asked me, as if it were the fruit of a problem long pondered in silence:

"If a sheep eats bushes, does it eat flowers, too?"

"A sheep eats whatever it finds."

"Even flowers that have thorns?"

"Yes. Even flowers that have thorns."

"Then what good are thorns?"

I didn't know. At that moment I was very busy trying to unscrew a bolt that was jammed in my engine. I was quite worried, for my plane crash was beginning to seem extremely serious, and the lack of drinking water made me fear the worst.

"What good are thorns?"

The little prince never let go of a question once he had asked it. I was annoyed by my jammed bolt, and I answered without thinking.

"Thorns are no good for anything—they're just the flowers' way of being mean!"

"Oh!" But after a silence, he lashed out at me, with a

sort of bitterness. "I don't believe you! Flowers are weak. They're naive. They reassure themselves whatever way they can. They believe their thorns make them frightening . . ."

I made no answer. At that moment I was thinking, *If this bolt stays jammed, I'll knock it off with the hammer.* Again the little prince disturbed my reflections.

"Then you think flowers . . ."

"No, not at all. I don't think anything! I just said whatever came into my head. I'm busy here with something serious!"

He stared at me, astounded.

"'Something serious'!"

He saw me holding my hammer, my fingers black with grease, bending over an object he regarded as very ugly.

"You talk like the grown-ups!"

That made me a little ashamed. But he added, mercilessly:

"You confuse everything . . . You've got it all mixed up!" He was really very annoyed. He tossed his golden curls in the wind. "I know a planet inhabited by a red-faced gentleman. He's never smelled a flower. He's never looked at a star. He's never loved anyone. He's never done anything except add up numbers. And all day long he says over and over, just like you, 'I'm a serious man! I'm a serious man!' And that puffs him up with pride. But he's not a man at all—he's a mushroom!"

"He's a what?"

"A mushroom!" The little prince was now quite pale with rage. "For millions of years flowers have been producing thorns. For millions of years sheep have been eating them all the same. And it's not serious, trying to understand why flowers go to such trouble to produce thorns that are good for nothing? It's not important, the war between the sheep and the flowers? It's no more serious and more important than the numbers that fat red gentleman is adding up? Suppose I happen to know a unique flower, one that exists nowhere in the world except on my planet, one that a little sheep can wipe out in a single bite one morning, just like that, without even realizing what he's doing—that isn't important?" His face turned red now, and he went on. "If someone loves a flower of which just one example exists among all the millions and millions of stars, that's enough to make him happy when he looks at the stars. He tells himself, 'My flower's up there somewhere . . .' But if the sheep eats the flower, then for him it's as if, suddenly, all the stars went out. And that isn't important?"

He couldn't say another word. All of a sudden he burst out sobbing. Night had fallen. I dropped my tools. What did I care about my hammer, about my bolt, about thirst and death? There was, on one star, on one planet, on mine, the Earth, a little prince to be consoled! I took him in my arms. I rocked him. I told him, "The flower you love is not in danger . . . I'll draw you a muzzle for your sheep . . . I'll draw you a fence for your flower . . . I . . ." I didn't know what to say. How clumsy I felt! I didn't know how to reach him, where to find him. . . . It's so mysterious, the land of tears.

VIII

I SOON LEARNED to know that flower better. On the little prince's planet, there had always been very simple flowers, decorated with a single row of petals so that they took up no room at all and got in no one's way. They would appear one morning in the grass, and would fade by nightfall. But this one had grown from a seed brought from who knows where, and the little prince had kept a close watch over a sprout that was not like any of the others. It might have been a new kind of baobab. But the sprout soon stopped growing and began to show signs of blossoming. The little prince, who had watched the development of an enormous bud, realized that some sort of miraculous apparition would emerge from it, but the flower continued her beauty preparations in the shelter of her green chamber, selecting her colors with the greatest care and dressing quite deliberately, adjusting her petals one by one. She had no desire to emerge all rumpled, like the poppies. She wished to appear only in the full radiance of her beauty. Oh yes, she was quite vain! And her mysterious adornment had lasted days and days. And then one morning, precisely at sunrise, she showed herself.

And after having labored so painstakingly, she yawned and said, "Ah! I'm hardly awake . . . Forgive me . . . I'm still all untidy . . ."

But the little prince couldn't contain his admiration.

"How lovely you are!"

"Aren't I?" the flower answered sweetly. "And I was born the same time as the sun . . ."

The little prince realized that she wasn't any too modest, but she was so dazzling!

"I believe it is breakfast time," she had soon added. "Would you be so kind as to tend to me?"

And the little prince, utterly abashed, having gone to look for a watering can, served the flower.

SHE HAD SOON begun tormenting him with her rather touchy vanity. One day, for instance, alluding to her four thorns, she remarked to the little prince, "I'm ready for tigers, with all their claws!"

"There are no tigers on my planet," the little prince had objected, "and besides, tigers don't eat weeds."

"I am not a weed," the flower sweetly replied.

"Forgive me . . ."

"I am not at all afraid of tigers, but I have a horror of drafts. You wouldn't happen to have a screen?"

"A horror of drafts . . . that's not a good sign, for a plant," the little prince had observed. "How complicated this flower is . . ."

"After dark you will put me under glass. How cold it is where you live—quite uncomfortable. Where I come from—" But she suddenly broke off. She had come here as a seed. She couldn't have known anything of other worlds. Humiliated at having let herself be caught on the verge of so naive a lie, she coughed two or three times in order to put the little prince in the wrong. "That screen?"

"I was going to look for one, but you were speaking to me!"

Then she made herself cough again, in order to inflict a twinge of remorse on him all the same.

SO THE LITTLE PRINCE, despite all the goodwill of his love, had soon come to mistrust her. He had taken seriously certain inconsequential remarks and had grown very unhappy.

"I shouldn't have listened to her," he confided to me one day. "You must never listen to flowers. You must look at them and smell them. Mine perfumed my planet, but I didn't know how to enjoy that. The business about the tiger claws, instead of annoying me, ought to have moved me . . ."

And he confided further, "In those days, I didn't understand anything. I should have judged her according to her actions, not her words. She perfumed my planet and lit up my life. I should never have run away! I ought to have realized the tenderness underlying her silly pretensions. Flowers are so contradictory! But I was too young to know how to love her."

IX

IN ORDER TO make his escape, I believe he took advantage of a migration of wild birds. On the morning of his departure, he put his planet in order. He carefully raked out his active volcanoes. The little prince possessed two active volcanoes, which were very convenient for warming his breakfast. He also possessed one extinct volcano. But, as he said, "You never know!" So he raked out the extinct volcano, too. If they are properly raked out, volcanoes burn gently and regularly, without eruptions. Volcanic eruptions are like fires in a chimney. Of course, on our Earth we are much too small to rake out our volcanoes. That is why they cause us so much trouble.

The little prince also uprooted, a little sadly, the last baobab shoots. He believed he would never be coming back. But all these familiar tasks seemed very sweet to him on this last morning. And when he watered the flower one last time, and put her under glass, he felt like crying.

"Good-bye," he said to the flower.

But she did not answer him.

"Good-bye," he repeated.

The flower coughed. But not because she had a cold.

He carefully raked out his active volcanoes.

"I've been silly," she told him at last. "I ask your forgiveness. Try to be happy."

He was surprised that there were no reproaches. He stood there, quite bewildered, holding the glass bell in midair. He failed to understand this calm sweetness.

"Of course I love you," the flower told him. "It was my fault you never knew. It doesn't matter. But you were just as silly as I was. Try to be happy . . . Put that glass thing down. I don't want it anymore."

"But the wind . . ."

"My cold isn't that bad . . . The night air will do me good. I'm a flower."

"But the animals . . ."

"I need to put up with two or three caterpillars if I want to get to know the butterflies. Apparently they're very beautiful. Otherwise who will visit me? You'll be far away. As for the big animals, I'm not afraid of them. I have my own claws." And she naively showed her four thorns. Then she added, "Don't hang around like this; it's irritating. You made up your mind to leave. Now go."

For she didn't want him to see her crying. She was such a proud flower. . . .

X

HE HAPPENED TO BE in the vicinity of Asteroids 325, 326, 327, 328, 329, and 330. So he began by visiting them, to keep himself busy and to learn something.

The first one was inhabited by a king. Wearing purple and ermine, he was sitting on a simple yet majestic throne.

"Ah! Here's a subject!" the king exclaimed when he caught sight of the little prince.

And the little prince wondered, *How can he know who I am if he's never seen me before?* He didn't realize that for kings, the world is extremely simplified: All men are subjects.

"Approach the throne so I can get a better look at you," said the king, very proud of being a king for someone at last.

The little prince looked around for a place to sit down, but the planet was covered by the magnificent ermine cloak. So he remained standing, and since he was tired, he yawned.

"It is a violation of etiquette to yawn in a king's presence," the monarch told him. "I forbid you to do so."

"I can't help it," answered the little prince, quite embarrassed. "I've made a long journey, and I haven't had any sleep . . ."

"Then I command you to yawn," said the king. "I haven't seen anyone yawn for years. For me, yawns are a curiosity. Come on, yawn again! It is an order."

"That intimidates me . . . I can't do it now," said the little prince, blushing deeply.

"Well, well!" the king replied. "Then I . . . I command you to yawn sometimes and sometimes to . . ."

He was sputtering a little, and seemed annoyed.

For the king insisted that his authority be universally respected. He would tolerate no disobedience, being an absolute monarch. But since he was a kindly man, all his commands were reasonable. "If I were to command," he would often say, "if I were to command a general to turn into a seagull, and if the general did not obey, that would not be the general's fault. It would be mine."

"May I sit down?" the little prince timidly inquired.

"I command you to sit down," the king replied, majestically gathering up a fold of his ermine robe.

But the little prince was wondering. The planet was tiny. Over what could the king really reign? "Sire . . . ," he ventured, "excuse me for asking . . ."

"I command you to ask," the king hastened to say.

"Sire . . . over what do you reign?"

"Over everything," the king answered, with great simplicity.

"Over everything?"

With a discreet gesture the king pointed to his planet, to the other planets, and to the stars.

"Over all that?" asked the little prince.

"Over all that . . . ," the king answered.

For not only was he an absolute monarch, but a universal monarch as well.

"And do the stars obey you?"

"Of course," the king replied. "They obey immediately. I tolerate no insubordination."

Such power amazed the little prince. If he had wielded it himself, he could have watched not forty-four but seventy-two, or even a hundred, even two hundred sunsets on the same day without ever having to move his chair! And since he was feeling rather sad on account of remembering his own little planet, which he had forsaken, he ventured to ask a favor of the king: "I'd like to see a sunset . . . Do me a favor, your majesty . . . Command the sun to set . . ."

"If I commanded a general to fly from one flower to the next like a butterfly, or to write a tragedy, or to turn into a seagull, and if the general did not carry out my command, which of us would be in the wrong, the general or me?"

"You would be," said the little prince, quite firmly.

"Exactly. One must command from each what each can perform," the king went on. "Authority is based first of all upon reason. If you command your subjects to jump in the ocean, there will be a revolution. I am entitled to command obedience because my orders are reasonable."

"Then my sunset?" insisted the little prince, who never let go of a question once he had asked it.

"You shall have your sunset. I shall command it. But I shall wait, according to my science of government, until conditions are favorable."

"And when will that be?" inquired the little prince.

"Well, well!" replied the king, first consulting a large calendar. "Well, well! That will be around . . . around . . . that will be tonight around seven-forty! And you'll see how well I am obeyed."

The little prince yawned. He was regretting his lost sunset. And besides, he was already growing a little bored. "I have nothing further to do here," he told the king. "I'm going to be on my way!"

"Do not leave!" answered the king, who was so proud of having a subject. "Do not leave; I shall make you my minister!"

"A minister of what?"

"Of . . . of justice!"

"But there's no one here to judge!"

"You never know," the king told him. "I have not yet explored the whole of my realm. I am very old, I have no room for a carriage, and it wearies me to walk."

"Oh, but I've already seen for myself," said the little prince, leaning forward to glance one more time at the other side of the planet. "There's no one over there, either . . ."

"Then you shall pass judgment on yourself," the king answered. "That is the hardest thing of all. It is much harder to judge yourself than to judge others. If you succeed in judging yourself, it's because you are truly a wise man."

"But I can judge myself anywhere," said the little prince. "I don't need to live here."

"Well, well!" the king said. "I have good reason to believe that there is an old rat living somewhere on my planet. I hear him at night. You could judge that old rat. From time to time you will condemn him to death. That way his life will depend on your justice. But you'll pardon him each time for economy's sake. There's only one rat."

"I don't like condemning anyone to death," the little prince said, "and now I think I'll be on my way."

"No," said the king.

The little prince, having completed his preparations, had no desire to aggrieve the old monarch. "If Your Majesty desires to be promptly obeyed, he should give me a reasonable command. He might command me, for instance, to leave before this minute is up. It seems to me that conditions are favorable . . ."

The king having made no answer, the little prince hesitated at first, and then, with a sigh, took his leave.

"I make you my ambassador," the king hastily shouted after him. He had a great air of authority.

"Grown-ups are so strange," the little prince said to himself as he went on his way.

XI

THE SECOND PLANET was inhabited by a very vain man.

"Ah! A visit from an admirer!" he exclaimed when he caught sight of the little prince, still at some distance. To vain men, other people are admirers.

"Hello," said the little prince. "That's a funny hat you're wearing."

"It's for answering acclamations," the very vain man replied. "Unfortunately, no one ever comes this way."

"Is that so?" said the little prince, who did not understand what the vain man was talking about.

"Clap your hands," directed the man.

The little prince clapped his hands, and the vain man tipped his hat in modest acknowledgment.

This is more entertaining than the visit to the king, the little prince said to himself. And he continued clapping. The very vain man continued tipping his hat in acknowledgment.

After five minutes of this exercise, the little prince tired of the game's monotony. "And what would make the hat fall off?" he asked.

But the vain man did not hear him. Vain men never hear anything but praise.

"Do you really admire me a great deal?" he asked the little prince.

"What does that mean—*admire?*"

"*To admire* means to acknowledge that I am the handsomest, the best-dressed, the richest, and the most intelligent man on the planet."

"But you're the only man on your planet!"

"Do me this favor. Admire me all the same."

"I admire you," said the little prince, with a little shrug of his shoulders, "but what is there about my admiration that interests you so much?" And the little prince went on his way.

"Grown-ups are certainly very strange," he said to himself as he continued on his journey.

XII

THE NEXT PLANET was inhabited by a drunkard. This visit was a very brief one, but it plunged the little prince into a deep depression.

"What are you doing there?" he asked the drunkard, whom he found sunk in silence before a collection of empty bottles and a collection of full ones.

"Drinking," replied the drunkard, with a
gloomy expression.

"Why are you drinking?" the little prince asked.

"To forget," replied the drunkard.

"To forget what?" inquired the little prince, who was
already feeling sorry for him.

"To forget that I'm ashamed," confessed the drunkard,
hanging his head.

"What are you ashamed of?" inquired the little prince,
who wanted to help.

"Of drinking!" concluded the drunkard, withdrawing
into silence for good. And the little prince went
on his way, puzzled.

"Grown-ups are certainly very, very strange," he said to himself as he continued on his journey.

XIII

THE FOURTH PLANET belonged to a businessman. This person was so busy that he didn't even raise his head when the little prince arrived.

"Hello," said the little prince. "Your cigarette's gone out."

"Three and two make five. Five and seven, twelve. Twelve and three, fifteen. Hello. Fifteen and seven, twenty-two. Twenty-two and six, twenty-eight. No time to light it again. Twenty-six and five, thirty-one. Whew! That amounts to five-hundred-and-one million, six-hundred-twenty-two thousand, seven hundred thirty-one."

"Five-hundred million what?"

"Hmm? You're still there? Five-hundred-and-one million . . . I don't remember . . . I have so much work to do! I'm a serious man. I can't be bothered with trifles! Two and five, seven . . ."

"Five-hundred-and-one million what?" repeated the little prince, who had never in his life let go of a question once he had asked it.

The businessman raised his head. "For the fifty-four years I've inhabited this planet, I've been interrupted only three times. The first time was twenty-two years ago, when I was interrupted by a beetle that had fallen onto my desk from god knows where. It made a terrible

noise, and I made four mistakes in my calculations. The second time was eleven years ago, when I was interrupted by a fit of rheumatism. I don't get enough exercise. I haven't time to take strolls. I'm a serious person. The third time . . . is right now! Where was I? Five-hundred-and-one million . . ."

"Million what?"

The businessman realized that he had no hope of being left in peace. "Oh, of those little things you sometimes see in the sky."

"Flies?"

"No, those little shiny things."

"Bees?"

"No, those little golden things that make lazy people daydream. Now, I'm a serious person. I have no time for daydreaming."

"Ah! You mean the stars?"

"Yes, that's it. Stars."

"And what do you do with five-hundred million stars?"

"Five-hundred-and-one million, six-hundred-twenty-two thousand, seven hundred thirty-one. I'm a serious person, and I'm accurate."

"And what do you do with those stars?"

"What do I do with them?"

"Yes."

"Nothing. I own them."

"You own the stars?"

"Yes."

"But I've already seen a king who—"

"Kings don't own. They 'reign' over . . . It's quite different."

"And what good does owning the stars do you?"

"It does me the good of being rich."

"And what good does it do you to be rich?"

"It lets me buy other stars, if somebody discovers them."

The little prince said to himself, *This man argues a little like my drunkard.* Nevertheless he asked more questions. "How can someone own the stars?"

"To whom do they belong?" retorted the businessman grumpily.

"I don't know. To nobody."

"Then they belong to me, because I thought of it first."

"And that's all it takes?"

"Of course. When you find a diamond that belongs to nobody in particular, then it's yours. When you find an island that belongs to nobody in particular, it's yours. When you're the first person to have an idea, you patent it and it's yours. Now I own the stars, since no one before me ever thought of owning them."

"That's true enough," the little prince said. "And what do you do with them?"

"I manage them. I count them and then count them again," the businessman said. "It's difficult work. But I'm a serious person!"

The little prince was still not satisfied. "If I own a scarf, I can tie it around my neck and take it away. If I own a flower, I can pick it and take it away. But you can't pick the stars!"

"No, but I can put them in the bank."

"What does that mean?"

"That means that I write the number of my stars on a slip of paper. And then I lock that slip of paper in a drawer."

"And that's all?"

"That's enough!"

That's amusing, thought the little prince. *And even poetic. But not very serious.* The little prince had very different ideas about serious things from those of the grown-ups. "I own a flower myself," he continued, "which I water every day. I own three volcanoes, which

I rake out every week. I even rake out the extinct one. You never know. It's of some use to my volcanoes, and it's useful to my flower, that I own them. But you're not useful to the stars."

The businessman opened his mouth but found nothing to say in reply, and the little prince went on his way.

"Grown-ups are certainly quite extraordinary" was all he said to himself as he continued on his journey.

XIV

THE FIFTH PLANET was very strange. It was the smallest of all. There was just enough room for a street lamp and a lamplighter. The little prince couldn't quite understand what use a street lamp and a lamplighter could be up there in the sky, on a planet without any people and not a single house. However, he said to himself, *It's quite possible that this man is absurd. But he's less absurd than the king, the very vain man, the businessman, and the drunkard. At least his work has some meaning. When he lights his lamp, it's as if he's bringing one more star to life, or one more flower. When he puts out his lamp, that sends the flower or the star to sleep. Which is a fine occupation. And therefore truly useful.*

When the little prince reached this planet, he greeted the lamplighter respectfully. "Good morning. Why have you just put out your lamp?"

"Orders," the lamplighter answered. "Good morning."

"What orders are those?"

"It's a terrible job I have."

"To put out my street lamp. Good evening." And he lit his lamp again.

"But why have you just lit your lamp again?"

"Orders."

"I don't understand," said the little prince.

"There's nothing to understand," said the lamplighter. "Orders are orders. Good morning." And he put out his lamp. Then he wiped his forehead with a red-checked handkerchief. "It's a terrible job I have. It used to be reasonable enough. I put the lamp out mornings and lit it after dark. I had the rest of the day for my own affairs, and the rest of the night for sleeping."

"And since then orders have changed?"

"Orders haven't changed," the lamplighter said. "That's just the trouble! Year by year the planet is turning faster and faster, and orders haven't changed!"

"Which means?"

"Which means that now that the planet revolves once a minute, I don't have an instant's rest. I light my lamp and turn it out once every minute!"

"That's funny! Your days here are one minute long!"

"It's not funny at all," the lamplighter said. "You and I have already been talking to each other for a month."

"A month?"

"Yes. Thirty minutes. Thirty days! Good evening." And he lit his lamp.

The little prince watched him, growing fonder and fonder of this lamplighter who was so faithful to orders. He remembered certain sunsets that he himself used to follow in other days, merely by shifting his chair. He wanted to help his friend.

"You know . . . I can show you a way to take a rest whenever you want to."

"I always want to rest," the lamplighter said, for it is possible to be faithful and lazy at the same time.

The little prince continued, "Your planet is so small that you can walk around it in three strides. All you have to do is walk more slowly, and you'll always be in the sun. When you want to take a rest just walk . . . and the day will last as long as you want it to."

"What good does that do me," the lamplighter said, "when the one thing in life I want to do is sleep?"

"Then you're out of luck," said the little prince.

"I am," said the lamplighter. "Good morning." And he put out his lamp.

Now that man, the little prince said to himself as he continued on his journey, *that man would be despised by all the others, by the king, by the very vain man, by the drunkard, by the businessman. Yet he's the only one who doesn't strike me as ridiculous. Perhaps it's because he's thinking of something besides himself.* He heaved a sigh of regret and said to himself, again, *That man is the only one I might have made my friend. But his planet is really too small. There's not room for two . . .*

What the little prince dared not admit was that he most regretted leaving that planet because it was blessed with one thousand, four hundred forty sunsets every twenty-four hours!

XV

THE SIXTH PLANET was ten times bigger than the last. It was inhabited by an old gentleman who wrote enormous books.

"Ah, here comes an explorer," he exclaimed when he caught sight of the little prince, who was feeling a little winded and sat down on the desk. He had already traveled so much and so far!

"Where do you come from?" the old gentleman asked him.

"What's that big book?" asked the little prince. "What do you do with it?"

"I'm a geographer," the old gentleman answered.

"And what's a geographer?"

"A scholar who knows where the seas are, and the rivers, the cities, the mountains, and the deserts."

"That is very interesting," the little prince said. "Here at last is someone who has a real profession!" And he gazed around him at the geographer's planet. He had never seen a planet so majestic. "Your planet is very beautiful," he said. "Does it have any oceans?"

"I couldn't say," said the geographer.

"Oh!" The little prince was disappointed. "And mountains?"

"I couldn't say," said the geographer.

"And cities and rivers and deserts?"

"I couldn't tell you that, either," the geographer said.

"But you're a geographer!"

"That's right," said the geographer, "but I'm not an

explorer. There's not one explorer on my planet.

A geographer doesn't go out to describe cities, rivers, mountains, seas, oceans, and deserts. A geographer is too important to go wandering about. He never leaves his study. But he receives the explorers there. He questions them, and he writes down what they remember. And if the memories of one of the explorers seem interesting to him, then the geographer conducts an inquiry into that explorer's moral character."

"Why is that?"

"Because an explorer who told lies would cause disasters in the geography books. As would an explorer who drank too much."

"Why is that?" the little prince asked again.

"Because drunkards see double. And the geographer would write down two mountains where there was only one."

"I know someone," said the little prince, "who would be a bad explorer."

"Possibly. Well, when the explorer's moral character seems to be a good one, an investigation is made into his discovery."

"By going to see it?"

"No, that would be too complicated. But the explorer is required to furnish proofs. For instance, if he claims to have discovered a large mountain, he is required to bring back large stones from it." The geographer suddenly grew excited. "But you come from far away! You're an explorer! You must describe your planet for me!"

And the geographer, having opened his logbook, sharpened his pencil. Explorers' reports are first recorded in pencil; ink is used only after proofs have been furnished.

"Well?" said the geographer expectantly.

"Oh, where I live," said the little prince, "is not very interesting. It's so small. I have three volcanoes, two active and one extinct. But you never know."

"You never know," said the geographer.

"I also have a flower."

"We don't record flowers," the geographer said.

"Why not? It's the prettiest thing!"

"Because flowers are ephemeral."

"What does *ephemeral* mean?"

"Geographies," said the geographer, "are the finest books of all. They never go out of fashion. It is extremely rare for a mountain to change position. It is extremely rare for an ocean to be drained of its water. We write eternal things."

"But extinct volcanoes can come back to life," the little prince interrupted. "What does *ephemeral* mean?"

"Whether volcanoes are extinct or active comes down to the same thing for us," said the geographer. "For us what counts is the mountain. That doesn't change."

"But what does *ephemeral* mean?" repeated the little prince, who had never in all his life let go of a question once he had asked it.

"It means, 'which is threatened by imminent disappearance.'"

"Is my flower threatened by imminent disappearance?"

"Of course."

My flower is ephemeral, the little prince said to himself, and she has only four thorns with which to defend herself against the world! And I've left her all alone where I live!

That was his first impulse of regret. But he plucked up his courage again. "Where would you advise me to visit?" he asked.

"The planet Earth," the geographer answered. "It has a good reputation."

And the little prince went on his way, thinking about his flower.

XVI

THE SEVENTH PLANET, then, was the Earth.

The Earth is not just another planet! It contains one hundred and eleven kings (including, of course, the African kings), seven thousand geographers, nine-hundred thousand businessmen, seven-and-a-half million drunkards, three-hundred-eleven million vain men; in other words, about two billion grown-ups.

To give you a notion of the Earth's dimensions, I can tell you that before the invention of electricity, it was necessary to maintain, over the whole of six continents, a veritable army of four-hundred-sixty-two thousand, five hundred and eleven lamplighters.

Seen from some distance, this made a splendid effect. The movements of this army were ordered like those of a ballet. First came the turn of the lamplighters of New Zealand and Australia; then these, having lit their street lamps, would go home to sleep. Next it would be the turn of the lamplighters of China and Siberia to perform their steps in the lamplighters' ballet, and then they too would vanish into the wings. Then came the turn of the lamplighters of Russia and India. Then those of Africa and Europe. Then those of South America, and of North America. And they never missed their cues for their appearances onstage. It was awe-inspiring.

Only the lamplighter of the single street lamp at the North Pole and his colleague of the single street lamp at the South Pole led carefree, idle lives: They worked twice a year.

XVII

TRYING TO BE WITTY leads to lying, more or less. What I just told you about the lamplighters isn't completely true, and I risk giving a false idea of our planet to those who don't know it. Men occupy very little space on Earth. If the two billion inhabitants of the globe were to stand close together, as they might for some big public event, they would easily fit into a city block that was twenty miles long and twenty miles wide. You could crowd all humanity onto the smallest Pacific islet.

Grown-ups, of course, won't believe you. They're convinced they take up much more room. They consider themselves as important as the baobabs. So you should advise them to make their own calculations—they love numbers, and they'll enjoy it. But don't waste your time on this extra task. It's unnecessary. Trust me.

So once he reached Earth, the little prince was quite surprised not to see anyone. He was beginning to fear he had come to the wrong planet, when a moon-colored loop uncoiled on the sand.

"Good evening," the little prince said, just in case.

"Good evening," said the snake.

"What planet have I landed on?" asked the little prince.

"On the planet Earth, in Africa," the snake replied.

"Ah! . . . And are there no people on Earth?"

"It's the desert here. There are no people in the desert. Earth is very big," said the snake.

The little prince sat down on a rock and looked up into the sky.

"I wonder," he said, "if the stars are lit up so that each of us can find his own, someday. Look at my planet—it's just overhead. But so far away!"

"It's lovely," the snake said. "What have you come to Earth for?"

"I'm having difficulties with a flower," the little prince said.

"Ah!" said the snake.

And they were both silent.

"Where are the people?" The little prince finally

The Little Prince was quite surprised not to see anyone.

resumed the conversation. "It's a little lonely in the desert . . ."

"It's also lonely with people," said the snake.

The little prince looked at the snake for a long time. "You're a funny creature," he said at last, "no thicker than a finger."

"But I'm more powerful than a king's finger," the snake said.

The little prince smiled.

"You're not very powerful . . . You don't even have feet. You couldn't travel very far."

"I can take you further than a ship," the snake said. He coiled around the little prince's ankle, like a golden bracelet. "Anyone I touch, I send back to the land from which he came," the snake went on. "But you're innocent, and you come from a star . . ."

The little prince made no reply.

"I feel sorry for you, being so weak on this granite earth," said the snake. "I can help you, someday, if you grow too homesick for your planet. I can—"

"Oh, I understand just what you mean," said the little prince, "but why do you always speak in riddles?"

"I solve them all," said the snake.

And they were both silent.

XVIII

THE LITTLE PRINCE crossed the desert and encountered only one flower. A flower with three petals—a flower of no consequence . . .

"You're a funny creature, no thicker than a finger."

"Good morning," said the little prince.

"Good morning," said the flower.

"Where are the people?" the little prince inquired politely.

The flower had one day seen a caravan passing.

"People? There are six or seven of them, I believe, in existence. I caught sight of them years ago. But you never know where to find them. The wind blows them away. They have no roots, which hampers them a good deal."

"Good-bye," said the little prince.

"Good-bye," said the flower.

XIX

THE LITTLE PRINCE climbed a high mountain. The only mountains he had ever known were the three volcanoes, which came up to his knee. And he used the extinct volcano as a footstool. *From a mountain as high as this one,* he said to himself, *I'll get a view of the whole planet and all the people on it . . .* But he saw nothing but rocky peaks as sharp as needles.

"Hello," he said, just in case.

"Hello . . . hello . . . hello . . . ," the echo answered.

"Who are you?" asked the little prince.

"Who are you . . . who are you . . . who are you . . . ," the echo answered.

"Let's be friends. I'm lonely," he said.

"I'm lonely . . . I'm lonely . . . I'm lonely . . . ," the echo answered.

What a peculiar planet! he thought. *It's all dry and sharp and hard. And people here have no imagination. They repeat whatever you say to them. Where I live I had a flower: She always spoke first . . .*

XX

BUT IT SO HAPPENED that the little prince, having walked a long time through sand and rocks and snow, finally discovered a road. And all roads go to where there are people.

"Good morning," he said.

It was a blossoming rose garden.

"Good morning," said the roses.

The little prince gazed at them. All of them looked like his flower.

"Who are you?" he asked, astounded.

"We're roses," the roses said.

"Ah!" said the little prince.

And he felt very unhappy. His flower had told him she was the only one of her kind in the whole universe. And here were five thousand of them, all just alike, in just one garden!

What a peculiar planet! It's all dry and sharp and hard.

She would be very annoyed, he said to himself, *if she saw this . . . She would cough terribly and pretend to be dying, to avoid being laughed at. And I'd have to pretend to be nursing her; otherwise, she'd really let herself die in order to humiliate me.*

And then he said to himself, *I thought I was rich because I had just one flower, and all I own is an ordinary rose. That and my three volcanoes, which come up to my knee, one of which may be permanently extinct. It doesn't make me much of a prince . . .* And he lay down in the grass and wept.

XXI

IT WAS THEN that the fox appeared.

"Good morning," said the fox.

And he lay down in the grass and wept.

"Good morning," the little prince answered politely, though when he turned around he saw nothing.

"I'm here," the voice said, "under the apple tree."

"Who are you?" the little prince asked. "You're very pretty . . ."

"I'm a fox," the fox said.

"Come and play with me," the little prince proposed. "I'm feeling so sad."

"I can't play with you," the fox said. "I'm not tamed."

"Ah! Excuse me," said the little prince. But upon reflection he added, "What does *tamed* mean?"

"You're not from around here," the fox said. "What are you looking for?"

"I'm looking for people," said the little prince. "What does *tamed* mean?"

"People," said the fox, "have guns and they hunt. It's quite troublesome. And they also raise chickens. That's the only interesting thing about them. Are you looking for chickens?"

"No," said the little prince, "I'm looking for friends. What does *tamed* mean?"

"It's something that's been too often neglected. It means, 'to create ties'. . ."

" 'To create ties'?"

"That's right," the fox said. "For me you're only a little boy just like a hundred thousand other little boys. And I have no need of you. And you have no need of me, either. For you I'm only a fox like a hundred thousand other foxes. But if you tame me, we'll need each other. You'll be the only boy in the world for me. I'll be the only fox in the world for you . . ."

"I'm beginning to understand," the little prince said. "There's a flower . . . I think she's tamed me . . ."

"Possibly," the fox said. "On Earth, one sees all kinds of things."

"Oh, this isn't on Earth," the little prince said.

The fox seemed quite intrigued. "On another planet?"

"Yes."

"Are there hunters on that planet?"

"No."

"Now that's interesting. And chickens?"

"No."

"Nothing's perfect," sighed the fox. But he returned to his idea. "My life is monotonous. I hunt chickens; people hunt me. All chickens are just alike, and all men are just alike. So I'm rather bored.

But if you tame me, my life will be filled with sunshine. I'll know the sound of footsteps that will be different from all the rest. Other footsteps send me back underground. Yours will call me out of my burrow like music. And then, look! You see the wheat fields over there? I don't eat bread. For me wheat is of no use whatever. Wheat fields say nothing to me. Which is sad. But you have hair the color of gold. So it will be wonderful, once you've tamed me! The wheat, which is golden, will remind me of you. And I'll love the sound of the wind in the wheat . . ."

The fox fell silent and stared at the little prince for a long while. "Please . . . tame me!" he said.

"I'd like to," the little prince replied, "but I haven't much time. I have friends to find and so many things to learn."

"The only things you learn are the things you tame," said the fox. "People haven't time to learn anything. They buy things ready-made in stores. But since there are no stores where you can buy friends, people no longer have friends. If you want a friend, tame me!"

"What do I have to do?" asked the little prince.

"You have to be very patient," the fox answered. "First you'll sit down a little ways away from me, over there, in the grass. I'll watch you out of the corner of my eye, and you won't say anything. Language is the source of misunderstandings. But day by day, you'll be able to sit a little closer . . ."

The next day the little prince returned.

"It would have been better to return at the same time," the fox said. "For instance, if you come at four in the afternoon, I'll begin to be happy by three. The closer it gets to four, the happier I'll feel. By four I'll be all excited and worried; I'll discover what it costs to be happy! But if you come at any old time, I'll never know when I should prepare my heart . . . There must be rites."

"What's a *rite?*" asked the little prince.

"That's another thing that's been too often neglected," said the fox. "It's the fact that one day is different from the other days, one hour from the other hours. My hunters, for example, have a rite. They dance with the village girls on Thursdays. So Thursday's a wonderful day: I can take a stroll all the way to the vineyards. If the hunters danced whenever they chose, the days would all be just alike, and I'd have no holiday at all."

THAT WAS HOW the little prince tamed the fox. And when the time to leave was near:

"Ah!" the fox said. "I shall weep."

"It's your own fault," the little prince said. "I never wanted to do you any harm, but you insisted that I tame you . . ."

"Yes, of course," the fox said.

"But you're going to weep!" said the little prince.

"Yes, of course," the fox said.

"Then you get nothing out of it?"

"I get something," the fox said, "because of the color of the wheat." Then he added, "Go look at the roses again.

"If you come at four in the afternoon, I'll begin to be happy by three."

You'll understand that yours is the only rose in all the world. Then come back to say good-bye, and I'll make you the gift of a secret."

THE LITTLE PRINCE went to look at the roses again.

"You're not at all like my rose. You're nothing at all yet," he told them. "No one has tamed you and you haven't tamed anyone. You're the way my fox was. He was just a fox like a hundred thousand others. But I've made him my friend, and now he's the only fox in all the world."

And the roses were humbled.

"You're lovely, but you're empty," he went on. "One couldn't die for you. Of course, an ordinary passerby would think my rose looked just like you. But my rose, all on her own, is more important than all of you together, since she's the one I've watered. Since she's the one I put under glass. Since she's the one I sheltered behind a screen. Since she's the one for whom I killed the caterpillars (except the two or three for butterflies). Since she's the one I listened to when she complained, or when she boasted, or even sometimes when she said nothing at all. Since she's *my* rose."

AND HE WENT back to the fox.

"Good-bye," he said.

"Good-bye," said the fox. "Here is my secret. It's quite simple: One sees clearly only with the heart. Anything essential is invisible to the eyes."

"Anything essential is invisible to the eyes," the little prince repeated, in order to remember.

"It's the time you spent on your rose that makes your rose so important."

"It's the time I spent on my rose . . . ," the little prince repeated, in order to remember.

"People have forgotten this truth," the fox said. "But you mustn't forget it. You become responsible forever for what you've tamed. You're responsible for your rose . . ."

"I'm responsible for my rose . . . ," the little prince repeated, in order to remember.

XXII

"GOOD MORNING," said the little prince.

"Good morning," said the railway switchman.

"What is it that you do here?" asked the little prince.

"I sort the travelers into bundles of a thousand," the switchman said. "I dispatch the trains that carry them, sometimes to the right, sometimes to the left."

And a brightly lit express train, roaring like thunder, shook the switchman's cabin.

"What a hurry they're in," said the little prince. "What are they looking for?"

"Not even the engineer on the locomotive knows," the switchman said.

And another brightly lit express train thundered by in the opposite direction.

"Are they coming back already?" asked the little prince.

"It's not the same ones," the switchman said. "It's an exchange."

"They weren't satisfied, where they were?" asked the little prince.

"No one is ever satisfied where he is," the switchman said.

And a third brightly lit express train thundered past.

"Are they chasing the first travelers?" asked the little prince.

"They're not chasing anything," the switchman said. "They're sleeping in there, or else they're yawning. Only the children are pressing their noses against the windowpanes."

"Only the children know what they're looking for," said the little prince. "They spend their time on a rag doll and it becomes very important, and if it's taken away from them, they cry..."

"They're lucky," the switchman said.

XXIII

"GOOD MORNING," said the little prince.

"Good morning," said the salesclerk. This was a salesclerk who sold pills invented to quench thirst. Swallow one a week and you no longer feel any need to drink.

"Why do you sell these pills?"

"They save so much time," the salesclerk said. "Experts have calculated that you can save fifty-three minutes a week."

"And what do you do with those fifty-three minutes?"

"Whatever you like."

"If I had fifty-three minutes to spend as I liked," the little prince said to himself, "I'd walk very slowly toward a water fountain . . ."

XXIV

IT WAS NOW the eighth day since my crash landing in the desert, and I'd listened to the story about the salesclerk as I was drinking the last drop of my water supply.

"Ah," I said to the little prince, "your memories are very pleasant, but I haven't yet repaired my plane. I have nothing left to drink, and I, too, would be glad to walk very slowly toward a water fountain!"

"My friend the fox told me—"

"Little fellow, this has nothing to do with the fox!"

"Why?"

"Because we're going to die of thirst."

The little prince didn't follow my reasoning, and answered me, "It's good to have had a friend, even if you're going to die. Myself, I'm very glad to have had a fox for a friend."

He doesn't realize the danger, I said to myself. *He's never hungry or thirsty. A little sunlight is enough for him . . .*

But the little prince looked at me and answered my thought. "I'm thirsty, too . . . Let's find a well . . ."

I made an exasperated gesture. It is absurd looking for a well, at random, in the vastness of the desert. But even so, we started walking.

WHEN WE HAD walked for several hours in silence, night fell and stars began to appear. I noticed them as in a dream, being somewhat feverish on account of my thirst. The little prince's words danced in my memory.

"So you're thirsty, too?" I asked.

But he didn't answer my question. He merely said to me, "Water can also be good for the heart . . ."

I didn't understand his answer, but I said nothing. . . . I knew by this time that it was no use questioning him.

He was tired. He sat down. I sat down next to him. And after a silence, he spoke again. "The stars are beautiful because of a flower you don't see . . ."

I answered, "Yes, of course," and without speaking another word I stared at the ridges of sand in the moonlight.

"The desert is beautiful," the little prince added.

And it was true. I've always loved the desert. You sit down on a sand dune. You see nothing. You hear nothing. And yet something shines, something sings in that silence. . . .

"What makes the desert beautiful," the little prince said, "is that it hides a well somewhere . . ."

I was surprised by suddenly understanding that mysterious radiance of the sands. When I was a little boy I lived in an old house, and there was a legend that a treasure was buried in it somewhere. Of course, no one was ever able to find the treasure, perhaps no one even searched. But it cast a spell over that whole house. My house hid a secret in the depths of its heart. . . .

"Yes," I said to the little prince, "whether it's a house or the stars or the desert, what makes them beautiful is invisible!"

"I'm glad," he said, "you agree with my fox."

As the little prince was falling asleep, I picked him up in my arms, and started walking again. I was moved. It was as if I was carrying a fragile treasure. It actually seemed to me there was nothing more fragile on Earth. By the light of the moon, I gazed at that pale forehead, those closed eyes, those locks of hair trembling in the wind, and I said to myself, *What I'm looking at is only a shell. What's most important is invisible . . .*

As his lips parted in a half smile, I said to myself, again, *What moves me so deeply about this sleeping little prince is his loyalty to a flower—the image of a rose shining within him like the flame within a lamp, even when he's asleep . . .* And I realized he was even more fragile than I had thought. Lamps must be protected: A gust of wind can blow them out. . . .

And walking on like that, I found the well at daybreak.

XXV

THE LITTLE PRINCE said, "People start out in express trains, but they no longer know what they're looking for. Then they get all excited and rush around in circles . . ." And he added, "It's not worth the trouble . . ."

The well we had come to was not at all like the wells of the Sahara. The wells of the Sahara are no more than holes dug in the sand. This one looked more like a village well. But there was no village here, and I thought I was dreaming.

"It's strange," I said to the little prince, "everything is ready: the pulley, the bucket, and the rope . . ."

He laughed, grasped the rope, and set the pulley working. And the pulley groaned the way an old weather vane groans when the wind has been asleep a long time.

"Hear that?" said the little prince. "We've awakened this well and it's singing."

I didn't want him to tire himself out. "Let me do that," I said to him. "It's too heavy for you."

He laughed, grasped the rope, and set the pulley working.

Slowly I hoisted the bucket to the edge of the well. I set it down with great care. The song of the pulley continued in my ears, and I saw the sun glisten on the still-trembling water.

"I'm thirsty for that water," said the little prince. "Let me drink some . . ."

And I understood what he'd been looking for!

I raised the bucket to his lips. He drank, eyes closed. It was as sweet as a feast. That water was more than merely a drink. It was born of our walk beneath the stars, of the song of the pulley, of the effort of my arms. It did the heart good, like a present. When I was a little boy, the Christmas-tree lights, the music of midnight mass, the tenderness of people's smiles made up, in the same way, the whole radiance of the Christmas present I received.

"People where you live," the little prince said, "grow five thousand roses in one garden . . . yet they don't find what they're looking for . . ."

"They don't find it," I answered.

"And yet what they're looking for could be found in a single rose, or a little water . . ."

"Of course," I answered.

And the little prince added, "But eyes are blind. You have to look with the heart."

I HAD DRUNK THE WATER. I could breathe easy now. The sand, at daybreak, is honey colored. And that color was making me happy, too. Why then did I also feel so sad?

"You must keep your promise," said the little prince, sitting up again beside me.

"What promise?"

"You know . . . a muzzle for my sheep . . . I'm responsible for this flower!"

I took my drawings out of my pocket. The little prince glanced at them and laughed as he said, "Your baobabs look more like cabbages."

"Oh!" I had been so proud of the baobabs!

"Your fox . . . his ears . . . look more like horns . . . and they're too long!" And he laughed again.

"You're being unfair, my little prince," I said. "I never knew how to draw anything but boas from the inside and boas from the outside."

"Oh, that'll be all right," he said. "Children understand."

So then I drew a muzzle. And with a heavy heart I handed it to him. "You've made plans I don't know about . . ."

But he didn't answer. He said, "You know, my fall to Earth . . . Tomorrow will be the first anniversary . . ." Then, after a silence, he continued. "I landed very near here . . ." And he blushed.

And once again, without understanding why, I felt a strange grief. However, a question occurred to me: "Then it wasn't by accident that on the morning I met you, eight days ago, you were walking that way, all alone, a thousand miles from any inhabited region? Were you returning to the place where you fell to Earth?"

The little prince blushed again.

And I added, hesitantly, "Perhaps on account . . . of the anniversary?"

The little prince blushed once more. He never answered questions, but when someone blushes, doesn't that mean "yes"?

"Ah," I said to the little prince, "I'm afraid . . ."

But he answered, "You must get to work now. You must get back to your engine. I'll wait here. Come back tomorrow night."

But I wasn't reassured. I remembered the fox. You risk tears if you let yourself be tamed.

XXVI

BESIDE THE WELL, there was a ruin, an old stone wall. When I came back from my work the next evening, I caught sight of my little prince from a distance. He was sitting on top of the wall, legs dangling. And I heard him talking. "Don't you remember?" he was saying. "This isn't exactly the place!" Another voice must have answered him then, for he replied, "Oh yes, it's the right day, but this isn't the place . . ."

I continued walking toward the wall. I still could neither see nor hear anyone, yet the little prince answered again: "Of course. You'll see where my tracks begin on the sand. Just wait for me there. I'll be there tonight."

I was twenty yards from the wall and still saw no one.

Then the little prince said, after a silence, "Your poison is good? You're sure it won't make me suffer long?"

I stopped short, my heart pounding, but I still didn't understand.

"Now go away," the little prince said. "I want to get down from here!"

Then I looked down toward the foot of the wall, and gave a great start! There, coiled in front of the little prince, was one of those yellow snakes that can kill you in thirty seconds. As I dug into my pocket for my revolver, I stepped back, but at the noise I made, the snake flowed over the sand like a trickling fountain, and without even hurrying, slipped away between the stones with a faint metallic sound.

I reached the wall just in time to catch my little prince in my arms, his face white as snow.

"What's going on here? You're talking to snakes now?"

I had loosened the yellow scarf he always wore. I had moistened his temples and made him drink some water. And now I didn't dare ask him anything more. He gazed at me with a serious expression and put his arms round my neck. I felt his heart beating like a dying bird's, when it's been shot. He said to me:

"I'm glad you found what was the matter with your engine. Now you'll be able to fly again . . ."

"How did you know?" I was just coming to tell him that I had been successful beyond all hope!

He didn't answer my question; all he said was "I'm leaving today, too." And then, sadly, "It's much further . . . It's much more difficult."

"Now go away . . . I want to get down from here!"

I realized that something extraordinary was happening. I was holding him in my arms like a little child, yet it seemed to me that he was dropping headlong into an abyss, and I could do nothing to hold him back.

His expression was very serious now, lost and remote. "I have your sheep. And I have the crate for it. And the muzzle . . ." And he smiled sadly.

I waited a long time. I could feel that he was reviving a little. "Little fellow, you were frightened . . ." Of course he was frightened!

But he laughed a little. "I'll be much more frightened tonight . . ."

Once again I felt chilled by the sense of something irreparable. And I realized I couldn't bear the thought of never hearing that laugh again. For me it was like a spring of fresh water in the desert.

"Little fellow, I want to hear you laugh again . . ."

But he said to me, "Tonight, it'll be a year. My star will be just above the place where I fell last year . . ."

"Little fellow, it's a bad dream, isn't it? All this conversation with the snake and the meeting place and the star . . ."

But he didn't answer my question. All he said was "The important thing is what can't be seen . . ."

"Of course . . ."

"It's the same as for the flower. If you love a flower that lives on a star, then it's good, at night, to look up at the sky. All the stars are blossoming."

"Of course . . ."

"It's the same for the water. The water you gave me

to drink was like music, on account of the pulley and the rope . . . You remember . . . It was good."

"Of course . . ."

"At night, you'll look up at the stars. It's too small, where I live, for me to show you where my star is. It's better that way. My star will be . . . one of the stars, for you. So you'll like looking at all of them. They'll all be your friends. And besides, I have a present for you." He laughed again.

"Ah, little fellow, little fellow, I love hearing that laugh!"

"That'll be my present. Just that . . . It'll be the same as for the water."

"What do you mean?"

"People have stars, but they aren't the same. For travelers, the stars are guides. For other people, they're nothing but tiny lights. And for still others, for scholars, they're problems. For my businessman, they were gold. But all those stars are silent stars. You, though, you'll have stars like nobody else."

"What do you mean?"

"When you look up at the sky at night, since I'll be living on one of them, since I'll be laughing on one of them, for you it'll be as if all the stars are laughing. You'll have stars that can laugh!"

And he laughed again.

"And when you're consoled (everyone eventually is consoled), you'll be glad you've known me. You'll always be my friend. You'll feel like laughing with me. And you'll open your window sometimes just for the fun of it . . . And your friends will be amazed to see you laughing while you're looking up at the sky. Then you'll tell them, 'Yes, it's the stars; they always make me laugh!' And they'll think you're crazy. It'll be a nasty trick I played on you . . ."

And he laughed again.

"And it'll be as if I had given you, instead of stars, a lot of tiny bells that know how to laugh . . ."

And he laughed again. Then he grew serious once more. "Tonight . . . you know . . . don't come."

"I won't leave you."

"It'll look as if I'm suffering. It'll look a little as if I'm dying. It'll look that way. Don't come to see that; it's not worth the trouble."

"I won't leave you."

But he was anxious. "I'm telling you this . . . on account of the snake. He mustn't bite you. Snakes are nasty sometimes. They bite just for fun . . ."

"I won't leave you."

But something reassured him. "It's true they don't have enough poison for a second bite . . ."

THAT NIGHT I didn't see him leave. He got away without making a sound. When I managed to catch up with him, he was walking fast, with determination. All he said was "Ah, you're here." And he took my hand. But he was still anxious. "You were wrong to come. You'll suffer. I'll look as if I'm dead, and that won't be true . . ."

I said nothing.

"You understand. It's too far. I can't take this body with me. It's too heavy."

I said nothing.

"But it'll be like an old abandoned shell. There's nothing sad about an old shell . . ."

I said nothing.

He was a little disheartened now. But he made one more effort.

"It'll be nice, you know. I'll be looking at the stars, too. All the stars will be wells with a rusty pulley. All the stars will pour out water for me to drink . . ."

I said nothing.

"And it'll be fun! You'll have five-hundred million little bells; I'll have five-hundred million springs of fresh water . . ."

And he, too, said nothing, because he was weeping. . . .

"HERE'S THE PLACE. Let me go on alone."

And he sat down because he was frightened.

Then he said:

"You know . . . my flower . . . I'm responsible for her. And she's so weak! And so naive. She has four ridiculous thorns to defend her against the world . . ."

And he sat down because he was frightened.

I sat down, too, because I was unable to stand any longer.

He said, "There . . . That's all . . ."

He hesitated a little longer, then he stood up. He took a step. I couldn't move.

There had been nothing but a yellow flash close to his ankle. He remained motionless for an instant. He didn't cry out. He fell gently, the way a tree falls. There wasn't even a sound, because of the sand.

XXVII

AND NOW, of course, it's been six years already. . . . I've never told this story before. The friends who saw me again were very glad to see me alive. I was sad, but I told them, "It's fatigue."

Now I'm somewhat consoled. That is . . . not entirely. But I know he did get back to his planet because at daybreak I didn't find his body. It wasn't such a heavy body. . . . And at night I love listening to the stars. It's like five-hundred million little bells. . . .

But something extraordinary has happened. When I drew that muzzle for the little prince, I forgot to put in the leather strap. He could never have fastened it on his sheep. And then I wonder, *What's happened there on his planet? Maybe the sheep has eaten the flower . . .*

Sometimes I tell myself, *Of course not! The little prince puts his flower under glass, and he keeps close watch over his sheep . . .* Then I'm happy. And all the stars laugh sweetly.

He fell gently, the way a tree falls. There wasn't even a sound. . . .

Sometimes I tell myself, *Anyone might be distracted once in a while, and that's all it takes! One night he forgot to put her under glass, or else the sheep got out without making any noise, during the night* . . . Then the bells are all changed into tears!

It's all a great mystery. For you, who love the little prince, too. As for me, nothing in the universe can be the same if somewhere, no one knows where, a sheep we never saw has or has not eaten a rose. . . .

Look up at the sky. Ask yourself, "Has the sheep eaten the flower or not?" And you'll see how everything changes. . . .

And no grown-up will ever understand how such a thing could be so important!

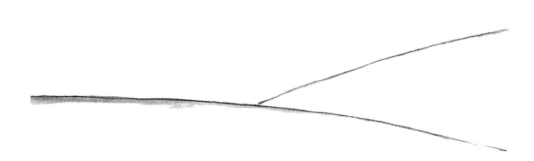

For me, this is the loveliest and the saddest landscape in the world. It's the same landscape as the one on the preceding page, but I've drawn it one more time in order to be sure you see it clearly. It's here that the little prince appeared on Earth, then disappeared.

Look at this landscape carefully to be sure of recognizing it, if you should travel to Africa someday, in the desert. And if you happen to pass by here, I beg you not to hurry past. Wait a little, just under the star! Then if a child comes to you, if he laughs, if he has golden hair, if he doesn't answer your questions, you'll realize who he is. If this should happen, be kind! Don't let me go on being so sad: Send word immediately that he's come back. . . .

Appreciations of
The Little Prince

The Little Prince's Universe
Characters and Planets

DELPHINE LACROIX
Researcher and historian specializing in
the history of *The Little Prince*

We always refuse to listen to our innocent inner self.
We suppress the child within who sees everything for the first time.
Paul Valéry, *Man and the Sea Shell,* Gallimard, 1937

Unlike most grown-ups, Saint-Exupéry didn't believe in having to explain himself.[1] This is why, whenever his little prince was asked a question, he "never provided an explanation." In fact, both author and hero felt that "anything essential is invisible to the eyes." This posture of theirs toward the world is one of the keys to understanding *The Little Prince* and to appreciating one of its fundamental lessons, that all things, animals, plants, and flowers are bound together by invisible ties. These bonds are not naturally occurring: they are forged via the processes of trade and through the establishment of culture and civilization. They enrich us and at the same time they impose a responsibility on us.

Each of the characters in *The Little Prince* is built on the notion that "man is nothing but a knot of relationships."[2] And because the nature of a relationship is such that it demands that one be able to listen and to share, there will always be some people who are destined to be alone, destined never to reap the benefits of genuine ties. A true relationship is an act of creativity, a fundamental component of life that allows us to make sense of it.

✳

THE AVIATOR

The story opens with a childhood memory: the narrator, as a child, is reading a book about the jungle, called *True Stories*. A scary picture in the book inspires him to take up pencil and paper and try his own hand at drawing. His first

1. "I have so little faith in explanations." Antoine de Saint-Exupéry, "Letter to Miss Lawton," in *Pilote de Guerre (Flight to Arras)* (Paris: Gallimard, 2013).

2. Antoine de Saint-Exupéry, *Citadelle (The Wisdom of the Sands),* in *Œuvres Complètes,* vol. II (Paris: Gallimard, 1999), p. 720.

The aviator in the desert, with his plane in the distance. Preparatory sketch not included in the final publication (1942).

drawing is of a boa constrictor swallowing an elephant. But when he shows it to grown-ups they fail to understand it and are unable to share in his excitement. When they fail to understand his second drawing, one that shows the elephant inside the boa, he gives up on ever having "a magnificent career as an artist," especially because everyone around him encourages him to apply himself instead to studying "geography, history, arithmetic, and grammar," all serious subjects.

Later, the narrator confesses that he's always held on to that drawing of the boa and the elephant, just in case he should ever run into a grown-up who seemed like he might understand. But he continues to be misunderstood. As he tells us this, he invites us to move beyond appearances, and to trust in our imagination so that we might come to have a sharper understanding of both the world and ourselves.

But the loneliness engendered by not having been understood endures, lingering on from one world to another, from the narrator's childhood into his adult years. Like the little prince who "needed a friend," the aviator "live[s] all alone, without anyone [he can] really talk to," until one day he meets this little fellow in the desert who actually does see the elephant inside the boa. And, thanks to his request, he starts to draw again. And, when he does so, he rediscovers the language of his childhood, the sense of urgency portrayed by drawings, and the sense of unity he had once felt between himself and the world.

The little prince and the aviator's hand. Preparatory sketch, 1942.

Through the bond of affection he forms with the little prince, the aviator rediscovers his old self. When they look for a well in the desert together, he remembers the buried treasure in his childhood home and is reminded of the "Christmas-tree lights, the music of midnight mass, the tenderness of people's smiles made up, in the same way, the whole radiance of the Christmas present [he'd] received." And this, in turn, leads him to understand that the "mysterious radiance of the sands" one sees in the desert is imparted not by the sand itself, but by our own capacity to grasp the true essence of things and what ties us to them over the course of time.

For his own part, the narrator's sense of self is informed by his *métier*: "I learned to pilot airplanes. I have flown almost everywhere in the world." Interestingly, an earlier version of the manuscript had him revealing more about himself: "For a long time I carried mail and passengers. [. . .] I even wrote books. And I fought in a war." Three additional drawings of the aviator are known to have existed, even if they were not included in the final version of the story. Two were of his hand holding a hammer—the tool he'll need to repair his plane—and the third was of him standing alone in the desert. But the final version of the book seems to downplay the aviator's importance by skipping over autobiographical details.

Of course, there can be no doubt that the narrator and the author are one and the same: the story is full of allusions to this effect. The strength of the

aviator lies in his ability to enter a dialogue with his own childhood, to meet again the creative child who represents the dawn of life. The aviator and the little prince might also be seen as two halves of the same character that hail from two different realities. And that character's echo carries on through the reader, who is invited to interpret its deeper meaning within the context of his own time.

✳

THE LITTLE PRINCE

"The act of painting a portrait is always driven by the idea of survival; it's an act of resistance against the ephemeral."
G. & P. Francastel, *Le Portrait*

We first encounter the little prince in Chapter II. Instead of naming him at the outset and then describing his character, Saint-Exupéry introduces the story's hero by way of his "funny little voice" and the unusual and urgent requests he makes of the aviator upon first meeting him. In fact, he isn't mentioned by name until the closing line of the chapter: "And that's how I made the acquaintance of the little prince." This rough outline is then fleshed out by degrees into the character that will go on to reflect, "I thought I was rich because I had just one flower, and all I own is an ordinary rose. That and my three volcanoes, which [only] come up to my knee, one of which may be permanently extinct. It doesn't make me much of a prince . . ."

From his first appearance at daybreak, the little prince's character is luminous and mysterious, Apollonian and radiant. His hair that is "the color of gold," the golden-yellow "scarf he always wore," and his stellar origins all combine to cast him in a golden aura: "But you're innocent, and you come from a star," the snake tells him. But he also has a dark side. The hidden melancholy reaches of his soul are revealed to us by his fondness for sunsets. For he loves entertaining himself by watching this daily disappearing act where sadness, love, and beauty are folded into one, and in the face of which we are at once reminded of our own mortality and made to yearn for eternity: "You know, when you're feeling very sad, sunsets are wonderful . . ."

If the best way to get to know someone is to understand what they want, the little prince is an easy study: he wants a drawing of a sheep. And while the reason he wants it remains mysterious at first, the urgency of his request is immediately clear. He asks for the drawing over and over and is satisfied only when he is finally given a drawing of a crate that holds the sheep. "That's just the kind I wanted!"

And yet, getting to know someone, even someone who is direct and straightforward, is a process. Each of the book's twenty-two illustrations of the little prince portray him in a different manner, almost as if he were a moving target, as if even a portrait of him could not capture his true nature: "One drawing works, and the next no longer bears any resemblance."

The best-known illustration is the one on the cover, where the little prince is shown standing on his planet, between two volcanoes and a handful of small flowers, staring into space with a faraway look: "His expression was very serious now, lost and remote." The most splendid illustration shows him in a princely costume, holding a sword. The caption reads: "Here is the best portrait I managed to make of him, later on." And the loveliest illustration is the one that appears on the title page, the one the narrator draws to show us how he believes the little prince left his planet. An excised passage from the book tells us "his eyes fell on the drawing of the flock of wild birds that carried him:—'That is the best picture. But that's not how I got here . . .'

He smiled with a sort of melancholy look:—'I can't tell you [about that,] it's my secret.'"

This may be why the first time they meet, the aviator is shocked to see that "this little fellow seemed to be neither lost nor dying of exhaustion, hunger, or thirst; nor did he seem scared to death." He observes the little prince carefully, and tries to deduce his secret, bit by bit. Through this process, the reader is invited to share in the aviator's discoveries, and to take the time to become acquainted with this little character who is worried, serious, and grave; who can turn "pale with rage," hold a grudge, be merciless, and grow very irritated, but who can also feel afraid, express regret, and, sometimes, feel let down. Gifted and sensitive, he is at once courageous and persistent, farseeing and intuitive. He takes his responsibilities seriously and applies discipline to taking good care of his planet, enjoying the sensation of a job well done.

This little prince can also cry, a trait that, especially in its tender spontaneity, distinguishes him from grown-ups and moves the narrator to draw the conclusion that "It's so mysterious, the land of tears." He also smiles and laughs: his laughter can awaken the universe because it transforms the stars into bells. His "peal of laughter" is like "a spring of fresh water in the desert" and a conduit to the entire universe: "When you look up at the sky at night, since I'll be living on one of them, since I'll be laughing on one of them, for you it'll be as if all the stars are laughing."

When the little fellow takes leave of the narrator, the tragedy of separation is revealed to us full-force. And yet, we also see how the power of a creative imagination can carry us through sorrow. The aviator can eventually come to "love listening to the stars" at night because they remind him of the little prince's laughter: "It's like five-hundred million little bells . . ." And when the fox whispers to the little prince—"But you have hair the color of gold. [. . .] The wheat, which is golden, will remind me of you. And I'll love the sound of the wind in the wheat . . ."—the bond of affection between them is forever cemented. The message survives because fields of wheat and the star-studded sky at night, that loveliest and saddest of all landscapes in the world, have the power to leave their mark on people. This is why, in the darkest moments of his own lifetime, Saint-Exupéry turned to his memories for solace: "All my memories, all my needs, all my loves are now available to me. My childhood, lost in darkness like a root, is at my disposal."[3]

3. Saint-Exupéry, *Pilote de Guerre (Flight to Arras)*, p. 184.

Drawing by Saint-Exupéry for his early poetry collection *The Adieu,* 1919.

FROM FLOWER TO ROSE

A flower isn't just something that blooms, opens up, and then fades. Such a description of a rose would be purely academic. It would kill a rose. A rose isn't a series of consecutive states of being, either. A rose is a sort of melancholic party.
Letter from Saint-Exupéry to Nelly de Vogüé, Orconte, France, December 1940

The rose is the reason the little prince has embarked on his journey: "What have you come to Earth for?" the snake asks him. "I'm having difficulties with a flower," the little prince answers. "Ah!" is the snake's laconic response, as if it already knows that the little prince will come to know the depth of his love for his flower only once they are apart; for when the rose and the little prince are together, there are misunderstandings between them that make them both miserable.

This is how we learn, in Chapter V, that, on his planet, the little prince is always on the lookout for any new twig that might sprout from the ground: whenever he sees one, he has to figure out if it is a baobab, which can be dangerous when it grows big, or a rosebush, as these plants closely resemble each other "when they're very young." We also find out that, on one occasion, while he was keeping watch, the little prince saw "a sprout that was not like any of the others. It might have been a new kind of baobab."

This leads into the little prince's explanation, in Chapter VII, of the tremendous significance of "the war between the sheep and the flowers." We learn that there exists a certain rose about which he is worried: his new friend, the sheep of the drawing, might eat it, despite its thorns. We come to know the flower in question: the rose and the little prince engage in a conversation and we learn how their relationship has unfolded. At first, the flower had prepared itself to appear in the world, in all its splendor, under the attentive and startled eye

of the little prince, who had not yet realized that this "miraculous apparition" was about to turn his world upside-down. "How lovely you are!" he had said to it, with great admiration. But it wasn't long before the flower's faults started to show: its lack of modesty, its prickly vanity, its lies and its craftiness. Fortunately, it was also capable of tenderness and "calm sweetness." As the little prince recounts this, he realizes that he had been "too young to know how to love [it]," that he should have looked at it and smelled it and not have listened to its words or silences, because language is a source of misunderstandings. Later in the story, when he meets the geographer and learns that his flower is ephemeral and perishable, he feels his first pang of remorse for having left it.

So, the great "secret of the little prince's life" is his love for a flower, a flower that, one day, will become "[his] rose." The flower is not identified as a rose until Chapter XX, in which the little prince discovers a blossoming rose garden. When he sees so many roses, it occurs to him that his own rose is just an ordinary rose among a million others, each one more beautiful than the last. At first, this discovery makes him unhappy, but it turns out he shouldn't be. For, thanks to the fox, who teaches him that it is the bond between him and his flower that is unique, the flower is transformed in his eyes into a rose: "I'm beginning to understand. [. . .] There's a flower . . . I think [it's] tamed me . . ."

The Little Prince's rose is both the ephemeral being that requires upkeep and protection, and to whose care he has dedicated so much time and attention, and the one through whom he comes to understand that a gift given can also be a gift received. It is because of the rose that he understands the fox's words: he understands what it means to feel a strong connection with someone and to therefore feel responsible[4] for them. He understands that, of all the roses in the universe, his rose is the only one he would single out, time after time, from any bouquet. For it is the one who spreads fragrance throughout his planet; it is love incarnate with all its joy, suffering, and beauty. It needs no justification; it is simply *there,* like love is.

The author's unusual relationship with his wife, Consuelo, would likely have resonated with the echoes of these sentiments. The two shared a complicated

4. For more on the notion of "responsibility," see Philippe Forest's essay "Each by Himself Is Responsible for All: The Morals of Saint-Exupéry" in *Pilote de Guerre: L'Engagement Singulier de Saint-Exupéry* (*Flight to Arras: A Singular Commitment*), edited by Delphine Lacroix (Gallimard Éditions, 2013).

life together, and one might imagine that when the little prince finally understands that his rose is unique, because he loves it, Saint-Exupéry has somehow reconciled himself to the circumstances of his own marriage.

Love, then, might be a *balm* that soothes man's ultimate loneliness, but more than anything it is a conduit: "The stars are beautiful because of a flower you don't see . . ." And yet, we sometimes forget how fairy tales can have cruel endings: "Maybe the sheep has eaten the flower . . ." Will the rose be devoured like the elephant was, despite its thorns, despite how well the little prince has taken care of it, despite its protective glass globe? Alas, the question will have to remain unanswered.

*

THE FOX

I'm raising either a fennec fox or a solitary fox. It's smaller than a cat and has huge ears. It's adorable. Unfortunately it's as wild as a beast and it snores like a lion!
Letter from Saint-Exupéry to his sister Didi, Cape Juby, Morocco, 1928

The image we have of animals has its roots in the depths of our imagination, in mythology and in the oral tradition of those medieval folktales in which the fox, the bear, the stag, the doe, and the bird often play crucial roles in their encounters with people and fairies. And storytellers have typically endowed these animals with a human voice, making their world the backdrop of the symbols they sow in their tales. Within this milieu, the fox occupies a singular position. It lives along the boundary between the human world and the wild one: it's neither entirely savage, nor can it be fully domesticated.

Like the little prince himself, the fox appears out of nowhere. Its arrival upon the scene might be said to mark a division of the story into two parts: the *before* and the *after*. For it will be the fox that reveals the story's fundamental lesson.

Why should it be a fox that delivers the most important message of the story? Because a fox is a figure to which children relate easily: it is jovial, understanding, and generous. It is intelligent, pragmatic, and mischievous; and it is charming and mysterious, to boot. It may not have the greatest opinion of people (the only things they are good at, in its mind, are raising chickens and dancing in the village), but this should come as no surprise since they do make a habit of hunting foxes. People, in the fox's opinion, are forgetful, impatient, and ignorant because they aren't willing to spend the time it takes to tame things. For this reason, they can never really get to know anything well; they miss out on the essential.

When you tame something, the fox teaches, you create a bond of affection with it: "But if you tame me, we'll need each other. You'll be the only boy in the world for me. I'll be the only fox in the world for you . . ." Things become special to us when we've invested in them, when we've taken the time to single them out, rescued them from the anonymity that comes of being one of a large number. And this is how something leaves its mark on us, breaks up the monotony of time, and gives meaning to our existence. To learn about friendship is to learn a sort of slow, choreographed dance. Finally, the fox delivers its biggest secret: "Anything essential is invisible to the eyes." And anyone able to see through this invisibility to the underlying bond that gives meaning to things will be the richer.

✳

THE SNAKE

Do they feel any differently now about the jungle growth and the
snakes? Before, they had been fused with something universal.
Saint-Exupéry, *Wind, Sand and Stars*

The snake is the first character we meet in *The Little Prince*. It is both fascinating and hypnotizing. We first see it "swallowing a wild beast"; then we see it from the "outside" and from the "inside." And in keeping with all respectable scenes of carnage, we are reminded that a snake like this "can kill you in thirty seconds," a warning in whose echo we can't help but be reminded of the swallowing of Europe by the Nazi regime. The snake is the first to welcome the little prince on Earth, and the one that will send him back to his planet, thereby defining the length of his journey.

Snakes are endowed with a dark power. They embody a metaphysical wisdom that allows them to solve the riddle of the beginning and end of things. They can go back and forth between the visible and invisible. Their power is sacred and knows no limits: they are "more powerful than a king's finger" and can "take you farther than a ship." Moreover, snakes have the power to inflict death on all beings: "Anyone I touch, I send back to the land from which he came." The snake in *The Little Prince* always speaks in riddles and always solves them.

Typewritten manuscript page from *The Little Prince*, 1942.

✳

THE SHEEP

When the aviator draws the sheep for the little prince, the sheep becomes the little prince's instant friend and will be forever treasured by him. For it has been a major preoccupation for him, the object of his dreams. Nevertheless, he has a lot of questions about this sheep. And as he rattles them off, the aviator gradually begins to understand him.

The sheep becomes the little prince's companion on Earth. But the little prince is also worried that his new friend might eat his rose, despite her thorns. So the aviator promises to draw him a muzzle. Alas, through their wanderings and curious discussions, he forgets to put in the leather strap on this second drawing for the little prince, an oversight that will leave him wondering, since the prince would not have been able to fasten the muzzle to the sheep, whether the sheep has "eaten the flower or not." He asks himself this, because he knows that all the bells in the sky will be "changed into tears" if that should happen. If anything should happen to that flower, then nothing in the whole universe will ever be the same.

✳

THE PLANETS, THE EARTH

The planets in *The Little Prince* are the setting for the unfolding drama of self-discovery. Their significance is perhaps best understood by reading Saint-

Exupéry's *Notebooks,* in which he writes that "men are like small human islands whose ability to react has been diminished."[5] This definition goes a long way toward helping us understand the suite of characters—the king, the vain man, the drunkard, the businessman, the lamplighter, and the geographer—that the little prince meets on his interplanetary travels.

Each of these characters follows a path leading nowhere and each ends up just chasing his own tail. They are all isolated. But, through their tail-chasing paths, each shows us that there is nothing more mysterious in a person than his propensity to feel satisfied with himself.[6]

The first of these characters we meet is a king, the one we are all familiar with from reading fairy tales, the one who wears an ermine cloak.[7] Since he has no subjects to rule over on his planet, he takes advantage of the little prince's visit to practice exercising his power. A king's world is very simple, you see. To him, "All men are subjects." He does not tolerate disobedience; he demands respect. But at the same time this king is also wise enough to know that "authority is based first of all upon reason," which is why he knows to pose this question to the little prince: "If I [were to command] a general to fly from one flower to the next like a butterfly, or to write a tragedy, or to turn into a seagull, and if the general did not carry out my command, which of us would be in the wrong, the general or me?"

The second character we meet is a "very vain man." This egomaniac spends all his time bowing to acknowledge acclamations and applause, like a puppet on strings. And since he hears nothing but praise, he is reduced to a life spent tipping his hat. When the little prince realizes that there is no place for anyone but the vain man on the planet, that he, himself, doesn't even exist in the vain man's eyes, he grows bored with the place and decides to leave. Later we learn that the vain man is the most representative of men on Earth.

The next character the little prince meets is the drunkard; this experience plunges him "into a deep depression." The drunkard is just turning in circles, drowning his sorrows in drink, and nothing seems capable of putting an end to it. He drinks to forget he is ashamed of drinking. The circle closes in on itself, locking the drunkard in a deep solitude.

On his next stop, the little prince meets a businessman. And though chances are the number of businessmen in the world is far greater today than it was in Saint-Exupéry's day, one can safely bet that their basic character has remained more or less the same. These men who sit about doing nothing but "add[ing] up numbers" are so self-important! The businessman whom the little prince meets

5. *Cahiers (Notebooks)*, 219, *Œuvres Complètes*, vol. I, p. 498.

6. Ibid., p. 616.

7. "Then, as if sharing a love of fairy tales, he added with an amused, knowing expression, 'Kings always wear ermine.'" Adèle Breaux, *Saint-Exupéry in America, 1942–1943: A Memoir* (1971).

A drunkard. Preparatory sketch, 1942.

is one who owns stars; he counts them and then counts them again, and then deposits them in the bank. It doesn't really matter to him whether he's of any use to his stars. His stars are lifeless stars. He will never experience that sense of satisfaction felt by a doctor, for example, or a teacher or a researcher, all of whom make a career of improving the life of the living. Through their work for others, these people make their own lives more meaningful, but the businessman, that "red-faced gentleman" who's "never smelled a flower," that mushroom puffed up with pride whose only preoccupation is profit, will never know the sweet feeling that comes from helping others.

The next character the little prince meets is the lamplighter; this one stands out from the others. "Perhaps it's because he's thinking of something besides himself." His planet revolves so fast (once per minute) that he is caught up in the endless task of lighting and then turning out his lamp, without ever taking a break. He does this because he's been ordered to do so and, even when the orders are inherently futile, he follows them faithfully. The full pathos of his character is highlighted by his inability to adapt to change, his robot-like determination to follow orders.

He is also the only one of the characters who gives of himself, for "When he lights his lamp, it's as if he's bringing one more star to life, or one more flower." And this incessant act, futile as it may be, is suffused with beauty; it makes it possible for the lamplighter to keep a small flame alive that, albeit obsolete, is a reminder of bygone times. His actions give meaning to the concept of "loyalty"[8] and dedication. That is why he is the only one the little prince could relate to, the only one he might have made his friend.

The next character the little prince meets is a geographer. This profession is one a pilot ought to be able to appreciate, but the constraints of this geographer's job are such that he isn't able to look about and see the beauty of the places around him for himself. He waits, instead, for explorers to come and give him an account of the details that will flesh out his maps.

The geographer is confined to his study, where he works cut off from the realities of the terrain he's studying. His scientific method is doubtful at best, and the proof he asks of explorers that come to him verges on the absurd. Perhaps the best way to understand the true nature of this geographer is to

8. In a letter to Joseph Kessel, Saint-Exupéry underlines the following words: "One must nourish the notion that 'loyalty' is, after all, the ability to recognize that the someone to whom one dedicates oneself completely is something bigger than one is oneself." Saint-Exupéry, *Œuvres Complètes*, vol. II, pp. 348–49.

A businessman? Preparatory sketch, 1942.

An explorer and a geographer?
Preparatory sketch, 1942.

reread the interesting geography lesson dispensed to Saint-Exupéry by his friend Guillaumet, the French aviator whose adventures he wrote about in his 1939 philosophical memoir *Wind, Sand and Stars:* "Under the light of the lamp, my map [of Spain] became a land of fairy tales. I marked the shelters and the traps with a cross. I marked the location of a farmer, a flock of thirty sheep, and a brook. I returned the shepherdess that had been neglected by geographers to her rightful spot on the map."

When he finally reaches Earth, the little prince meets other men, a railway switchman and a merchant of pills. There are no illustrations of these characters, but their presence highlights the absurdity of the human condition, slave as it is to advances in technology and to the so-called development of civilization. From his train compartment, the railway switchman sees travelers moving in bundles of a thousand, "sometimes to the right, sometimes to the left." These people travel without any purpose; they're not even pursuing a destination that might give meaning to their existence. They are reminiscent of the "commuter train" people of Saint-Exupéry's *Wind, Sand and Stars,* whose lives, with their stifling rituals, are reduced to an ant-like existence. Today, when the sole purpose of a man's life is reduced to consuming and producing, he has no true path to guide him, and it is as if he has no roots. "People start out in the express trains, but they no longer know what they are looking for. Then they get all excited and rush around in circles . . ." And as far as the pill merchant is concerned, he sells a lot of nothing, in the name of progress. All meaning is lost and there is nothing to show people a happy way of life.[9] They are alone and spin around in circles. Or, as the rose in the desert tells the little prince, "The wind blows them away."

9. "There is no freedom but the freedom of someone who is going somewhere. Such a man can be set free if you will teach him the meaning of thirst and show him the way to a well. Only then will he embark on a course of action that isn't meaningless." Saint-Exupéry, *Pilote de Guerre* (*Flight to Arras*), in *Œuvres Complètes,* vol. II, p. 217.

THE REVELATION OF THE BOND OF AFFECTION

Reverie works in a star pattern.
Gaston Bachelard, *The Psychoanalysis of Fire*

Through the little prince's odyssey, we are introduced to a great many peculiar things. We learn about the little prince's planet, his three volcanoes—one of which may be extinct forever— and his rose. We learn about a planet inhabited by a single lazy person whose idleness threatens the planet's very existence; we learn about the planets where various men live; and, finally, we learn about Earth. This last planet seems quite inhospitable to the little prince, for he is hard put to find anyone there. But he does meet a snake and a desert flower, and then he crosses "sand and rocks and snow" until he finally discovers a road, and then a garden, both signs that Earth is indeed inhabited by people. He speaks with the roses in the garden and tells them that, although they are very lovely, they are empty. And he meets the fox that will eventually reveal to him the secret of the importance of invisible bonds. In the end, however, it isn't the people he meets who will be responsible for his great awakening, but rather the fauna and the flora. For unlike his experience with people, the little prince is able to engage with them. When he calls out for people and friends, the only response he gets is in the form of a mysterious echo calling "I'm lonely . . . I'm lonely . . . I'm lonely."

Such an experience would have been familiar to Saint-Exupéry, who, after his plane had crashed a few years earlier, had journeyed a long way across the desert looking for a well or anyone who might give him something to drink. It would also be familiar because he'd heard firsthand of the ordeal of his friend Guillaumet, who had trekked through the snowy peaks of the Andes looking for help after his plane had crashed in South America. These experiences had reminded the author that in these extreme situations, a call for help could mean the difference between life and death.

For him, a well in the desert is the ultimate symbol of the grail. The water drawn from a well can restore a man to his true human dimensions. In *The Wisdom of the Sands,* Saint-Exupéry writes: "I say that if a well is well-built and sings in your heart, once you've become one with the sand and are ready to free yourself of your outer shell, it will offer you peaceful water that isn't the thing itself, but the essence of the thing, and I'd still be able to get you

Winged figure. Preparatory sketch, 1942.

10. Saint-Exupéry, *Terre des Hommes* (*Wind, Sand and Stars*), in *Œuvres Complètes,* vol. I, p. 205; "I went to see my plane this evening," in Antoine de Saint-Exupéry, *Manon Danseuse et Autres Textes Inédits* (*Manon Ballerina and Other Unpublished Works*) (Paris: Gallimard, 2007), pp. 46–50.

11. Saint-Exupéry loved to draw comparisons between men and trees. "Planted in the Earth by its roots, planted among the stars by its branches, the tree is the means through which man communicates with the stars." Saint-Exupéry, *Citadelle* (*The Wisdom of the Sands*), in *Œuvres Complètes,* vol. II, p. 401.

12. Saint-Exupéry, *Terres des Hommes* (*Wind, Sand and Stars*), in *Œuvres Complètes,* vol. I, p. 274.

to smile by telling you how sweet the singing of a well can be."

A well imparts radiance to the desert much as a hidden buried treasure lends its sheen to a childhood home. Why is this important? Because these invisible treasures, these reserves of sweetness, have the power to transform a person who has come face to face with death; they establish an unbreakable bond with him that is absolute, boundless. Only intuition can come close to it in the ability to make one feel so connected with the world and the universe.

This connection with the universe is one of Saint-Exupéry's signature themes. In *Wind, Sand and Stars,* he describes coming across some stony meteorites ("black stones as hard as diamonds") and refers to the sky as a celestial apple tree[10] from which the dust of stars falls like apples to the Earth. This is proof, he writes, that we who inhabit the Milky Way are part of a greater cosmos. And this image, like the image of the fox imparting words of wisdom "under the apple tree" in *The Little Prince,* brings us closer to an understanding of man's primordial relationship with the universe. A network of connections starts to take shape before our eyes.

This is the human drama *The Little Prince* invites us to participate in, far away from profit-and-loss calculations, far away from bridge parties and disputes. In this sense, what Saint-Exupéry is after is reconciliation. What he wants is to bring us back into the fold of community. He does this by inviting us to listen to the world's prose, so that we might see that a flower is a star and a star is a flower, so that we might see that the apple tree isn't just a ladder into the sky, but an invitation to partake of its fruit.[11] Even migrating birds, he tells us, participate in this great invisible drama: "As if magnetized by the great triangular flight, the barnyard fowls leap a foot or two into the air and try to fly. The call of the wild strikes them with the force of a harpoon and a vestige of savagery quickens their blood. All the ducks on the farm have, for a moment, become migratory birds. And, behold, the humble thoughts of ponds, worms, and poultry houses that previously preoccupied their small brains, have been supplanted by loftier thoughts about vast expanses of continents and by the taste for onshore winds, and the vast array of oceans."[12]

Indeed, it is the great expanse itself that beckons them to migrate, just as it lures a person into exploring the open seas to discover places he might become connected to. This vast expanse is the guiding principle whereby we understand rituals, friendship, love, the invisible, all the hidden attractions. The author delivers this message in *Flight to Arras* as well: "True expanses are not matters for the eye; they are visible only to the soul. They are only as valuable as the words used to describe them; for it is language that ties things together. [. . .] These vast expanses are not to be found. They have to be created."

Great expanses, like a poem, then, like *The Little Prince,* in fact, build a language of their own, and this language, in turn, creates emotion.

The concept of the bond that ties the things of this world together generates its own theory of the origin of the universe: it organizes the structure of language and the universe on the basis of a series of analogies. In the heart of the desert, a "secret set of living muscles" responds to the "network of trails, hills, and signs" toward which everything seems to point.

The Little Prince itself creates a bond of affection with the reader, a bond that evolves over time. It invites us to reconsider what it is that ties us to the world. In fact, it is precisely the type of book Saint-Exupéry had always dreamed of reading, a book that can "quench [man's] thirst."[13]

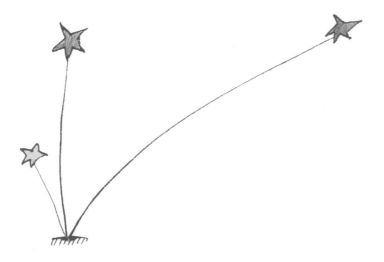

13. "The heart needs other employment. [. . .] The only refreshing spring I can find is in some childhood memories: the smell of burning candles on Christmas Eve. Nowadays it's the soul that is a desert, dying of thirst. I have time to write, but I'm not ready to, the book hasn't yet matured inside me—a book that should quench thirst." Antoine de Saint-Exupéry, letter to his mother, Orconte, 1940, in *Œuvres Complètes,* vol. I, p. 849.

Themes of The Little Prince

VIRGIL TĂNASE
French-Romanian writer,
translator, and philosopher

In the middle of the desert, a "thousand miles from any inhabited country," a stranded aviator-narrator prepares to undertake the difficult task of repairing his downed plane. This is how *The Little Prince* begins. But, interesting as the story line promises to be, it will figure so insignificantly in the story that unfolds in the pages that follow, that one can't help wondering whether the accident was invented as a pretext to take the reader someplace where the narrator could be alone with his thoughts. For the next morning, as if still in a dream, the aviator is awakened from sleep by a most "extraordinary little fellow" who doesn't come to advise him on a rescue plan, or to offer mechanical assistance, but, rather, to ask him to draw him a sheep. The request causes the narrator to remember a time when, as a child, he'd been looking at a picture in a book about the jungle and had drawn a boa constrictor; when he'd shown it to the "grown-ups" around him, they'd mistaken it for a hat.

But what would have happened if instead of being a budding artist as a child, the narrator had fancied himself a writer, and instead of showing the grown-ups a picture of a boa, he had shown them the story of *The Little Prince*? Then, when his plane had broken down in the desert, it might have been a story, not a picture, that he would have recollected and submitted to the critical eye of this little fellow whom he so resembled (especially in his use of direct questions to cut what grown-ups refer to as "Gordian knots").

"It's a story about a man who is who he isn't," the little prince would have said to the aviator, when he'd read it.

"Excuse me?"

"Yes, the theme or, rather, what wise men on this planet refer to as the

The little prince, as seen by the aviator. Sketch, 1942.

'theme,' . . . the theme of this short story that prompted so many grown-ups to advise you to abandon writing so that you could focus on science instead, learn how to work with numbers, and how to fly a plane . . . the theme of this story that is told like a fairy tale is that 'man is what he isn't.' It's crystal clear, patently obvious! There's no need to go inventing fifty new planets just to disguise, with some fancy scheme, what can be seen with the naked eye . . ."

So, let's consider, what is the message the author wants to convey with this story that at first glance appears to be as simple as its illustrations? Is it really about an aviator who is stranded in the desert and then sees a child appear out of thin air who tells him about his interplanetary travels and some of the characters he meets on Earth? Is it about a railway switchman, some roses, a merchant of pills, a fox, or a snake? And aren't the narrator and the little fellow so like-minded, don't they share so many traits in the depths of their souls, that one can't help wonder if they might be one and the same? And if that is the case, why do they both have to be in the story? For the simple reason, as we've just been told, that "man is what he isn't."

*

So, *who* is he? How can we see him in his unadulterated form? Strange as it may seem, "all grown-ups were children first," but they don't stay children for long, which is really a pity. So, what becomes of them? What becomes of the children that once were? This theme is one with which Saint-Exupéry had long been preoccupied, even before he wrote *The Little Prince.* Once while traveling by train from Paris to Moscow, he had been so taken by a family of Polish laborers he'd met in the third-class carriage that he had written about them in his journal: they'd been sent back from France after running out of work. When he first saw them, they were asleep. Their worn-out faces, he remarked in his notes, were testament to a life of misery that had turned them into pack animals. But the little boy who slept in his mother's arms had an angelic face and, Saint-Exupéry felt, might have had the makings of a Mozart. He also remarked, however, that the moment that child entered adulthood he'd be subjected to the constraints of a vulgar existence, to the trials and tribulations of grown-up society and, as a result, was unlikely to go on to compose any symphonies. So would the child's innocence and promise just be "obliterated"? "No," the author emphasized in his notes. "No," they wouldn't. The innocent child would always remain "trapped" within. Each of us has a child trapped within, he noted, and our mission should be to *awaken* it. We mustn't abandon or forget it; we mustn't allow this society that will soon be able to mass-produce pianos in an assembly line, but be incapable of producing a musician,[1] to wipe out the miraculous seed each one of us carries within, from birth. The greatest challenge of our lives is to let ourselves be guided by this unblemished side, this part of us that is so much like a precious jewel securely stored away in a box.

1. John Phillips, "On the night of May 29th," *Icare*, no. 96, p. 131.

*

The first question one might ask, then, is *Why should one be guided by the child within? Why not grow up? Why not march on into adulthood without any hesitation?* The author offers multiple reasons that highlight the qualities of adults that are absent in children.

"Grown-ups" judge according to appearances: This is why, for example, they don't believe in the existence of Asteroid B-612, the one the little prince supposedly hailed from. They won't lend any credibility to its discovery for the simple reason that the Turkish astronomer who reports its existence is dressed in Oriental garb when he presents his findings; his discovery cannot possibly be credible unless he is dressed in Western clothes when he presents it. If they want to get to know somebody, grown-ups are interested in only superficial details about them; they want to know, "How old is he?" "How many brothers does he have?" "How much does he weigh?" "How much money does his father make?" And a grown-up geographer (like the one the little prince meets on his journeys) who needs to know the physiography of his planet won't go out to look at it himself but, rather, will be content to hear about it secondhand from his explorers; he will draw his conclusions about the size of a mountain on the basis of the size of a rock from that mountain.

Sketch, 1942.

"Grown-ups" come up with all kinds of excuses for doing things they know are not right: the drunkard regrets that he is a drunkard, but drinks "to forget" his shame, which seems a good solution to him because it is pleasurable.

"Grown-ups" are vain: They'll go to any length to make themselves admired and will even accept empty flattery to fool themselves into believing they are important. Such is the way of the king whom the little prince meets. To convince himself that he is so

powerful that even the sun obeys him, he orders it to rise in the morning and to set in the evening.

"Grown-ups" are greedy: They amass goods and they end up wanting to own everything, even if it is only in theory, even if it is something that is beyond their grasp and of no use at all. Such is the case with the businessman—the "awful American businessman"[2]—whom the little prince meets. He spends his life counting the stars he thinks he "owns" because he is the first to have thought of owning them, and since no one else ever thought of owning them, before, they must be his. He writes the number of "his" stars on a slip of paper and deposits it in the bank.

"Grown-ups" don't have roots: They are blown around by the wind. They board trains by the thousands without even knowing why, without knowing where they want to go. "Grown-ups" don't know what they are looking for so they "stagger about and turn in circles."

"Grown-ups" lack imagination: When they look at a drawing of a boa that has swallowed an elephant, all they see is a hat. They are incapable of realizing that things might be different from what they seem. They are incapable of realizing that man, too, "isn't what he is" or, if you prefer, "is what he isn't."

✳

Plenty of good reasons to never grow up, one might conclude. But, then, one might ask, *what is it about childhood that so fascinated Saint-Exupéry?* His work sheds abundant light on the subject. To begin with, he admired the extraordinary ability children have of understanding right away that what might *seem like a hat* isn't actually a hat; he admired the fact that, unlike almost everyone else, children always know exactly what they want. These qualities might not be that extraordinary in and of themselves, if it were not that they reflect a deeper meaning that is likely the real focus of the story: every person was a child before becoming an adult and, in fact, the child is always there, even when, one day, the person grows up and thinks himself special in the hectic and vain world of grown-ups; and, more surprising still, that inner child lives on even when the physical body throws in the towel and dies, returning to dust.

The formula that unlocks the mystery of life, in other words, is of biblical simplicity. The bundle of flesh that grows up, becomes an adult, and dies is but an expression of the greater, immortal being within, the Spirit, which is held by the Creator between two extremes that we don't quite understand (one would be mistaken to believe that because he wasn't a practicing Christian, Saint-Exupéry

2. For more on the subject, see Antoine de Saint-Exupéry, *Carnets* (*Notebooks*), in *Œuvres Complètes,* vol. I, (Paris: Gallimard, 1994), p. 562.

was not a deeply spiritual man). Although this is regrettable, it doesn't change the fact that creation makes sense and all one has to do to be part of the great truth is let oneself be carried by this breath that moves through us and that, for lack of any better name, we call *Spirit*. And so that we might see it in the flesh, we might personify this Spirit in the form of a child.

Let's not forget, however, that this child who, by all accounts, is the author himself, or at least a part of him, is a little "prince." He is endowed with a royal title. And a noble title is something that lasts forever, that is passed on from one generation to the next, regardless of whether the bearer's behavior has been cowardly or heroic. To be *noble* means to be the current bearer of an ancient tradition of obligation and responsibility that will continue to live on long after the bearer has died. The theme of *The Little Prince,* or what wise men on this planet refer to as the "theme," then, becomes evident: *man and Spirit are one and the same.* We live in a world of which one part, the "shell," is ephemeral, "threatened by imminent disappearance," while another part lives on.

✳

The author's preoccupation with this theme is evident elsewhere in his work as well. In one of his notebooks, he writes a series of questions: What is the meaning of *civilization?* Is it not the desire to "hold on to our heritage"?[3] And what is the meaning of *Spirit?* Is it not our desire to preserve and look after the things we have loved? Isn't it a faithful adherence to traditions whose substance, in the end, isn't even as important as the commitment to keeping them alive? Or is it the case, instead, that the substance of traditions is *the act of preservation itself,* much as it is the substance of civilizations?

Surely we know that all things, whether good or bad, come to an end, and we don't have it in our power to prevent them from doing so. But in one thing we are constant, and that is in our loyalty and devotion. The mood swings of the rose that drive the little prince from his planet are circumstantial; and the rose itself is vulnerable: a little sheep might eat it . . . Our hero's devoted affection for the rose, by contrast, is rock solid. It means so much to the little prince, that the emotional bond he feels for it supersedes any fear of death. "Your poison is good?" he asks the snake that will help deliver him of his overly "heavy" body. "You're sure it won't make me suffer long?" Perhaps, once rid of his body, he'll be better able to travel from one planet to another (the last time he'd left his planet, he'd had to hitch a ride with a flock of wild birds). Perhaps he'll be better equipped not only to find his rose again, but also to carry out what he sees as his duty, to assume eternal responsibility for it, the one with whom he shares an

3. Ibid., p. 565.

emotional bond, the flower that is unique among all flowers and that we now know is the embodiment of the Spirit.

*

You might be asking yourself—well, maybe not you, personally, but grown-ups like me who feel the need to explain what doesn't really need any explanation, just to cover up their own sense of inadequacy—you might be asking yourself what, exactly, is the nature of this "emotional bond" that approximates Saint-Exupéry's concept of the Spirit? As chance has it, it isn't a person who will answer this question, but a fox. And its revelation should not be taken lightly. This type of affection, it tells us, isn't the type one feels when one falls head over heels for someone. No, it is a feeling that develops slowly; it is a choice we make that introduces a sense of order in an otherwise chaotic world. It is a choice that might have been arbitrary—it doesn't matter whether it was haphazard or not—but that nevertheless creates order out of chaos. For, after all, that is what *cosmos* is: it is everlasting order. It might not seem like this amounts to much until, one day, a little fox, taking its clue from Providence who created the Earth out of the void, teaches a little prince how to make a friend; how, by having patience, one might earn someone's trust; or how one can become so indispensable to someone that that person's days can go from being dull to being full of expectation just by his knowing that the friend will be coming to him. It might not seem like much until it teaches him (and us) how to arrange the disparate events of his life into a destiny.

Emotional bond and Spirit, in this sense, are one and the same, but forming an emotional bond isn't easy: it requires effort. And this effort is precisely what the Spirit *is*. Spirit is the willingness to look for a spring, or to dig a well when one is thirsty instead of just inventing a pill that will quench one's thirst. "That water was more than merely a drink," said the aviator. "It was born of our walk between the stars, of the song of the pulley, of the effort of my arms. It did the heart good, like a present."

*

Yes, the Spirit, we now understand, is not a divine revelation, but a person's capacity to gift himself a horizon to steer by and stay the course. Spirit is what makes a person a person. Or, more precisely, it is what makes each person an individual, a unique reality in the infinite universe. For when they are all amassed, Saint-Exupéry tells us people are like ants in an anthill, a conglomerate of physical beings that live by following a set of preordained rules. He is a pebble

Il etait triste et donc
injuste, j'ai banni tout
ce qu'il disait...
mais j'ai gardé le
dessin parce qu'il est
tellement ressemblant...

Il n'est pas si méchant que ça, mais il est
tellement melancolique...

A.

"He was sad and, as a
result, unfair. I blocked out
everything he said . . . but I
kept the drawing because it
looks so much like him . . . /
He's really not as mean as
that; he's just so sad . . . / A."
Letters to a Stranger, Algeria,
1943–44.

that surrenders to the forces of gravity. Our Spirit, which allows us to dream and to create, is immune to these forces and is subject to another set of laws, laws beyond the reach of the temporary body in which it dwells.

"What," asks the author who in 1944 caricatured life in America in the form of a businessman, "will remain of our civilization when all that is spiritual has been annihilated? What will remain of us if we fail to learn to elevate our aspirations to something greater than the mechanical monstrosities our engineers come up with?"[4] It is imperative that we allow the individual within us, the Spirit, to affirm itself. It is imperative that we allow our essence to prevail. These are some of the themes the author explores in *The Little Prince.*

The essence of an individual is, after all, the quality that he alone possesses and shares with no one else in the universe. It is what distinguishes him, say, from the sun, the beasts, a Frigidaire, Buicks, sewing machines, and the plants Saint-Exupéry would have liked to look after ("I should have been a gardener," he said near the end of his life, "not an aviator or a writer, but a gardener!"[5]). It is the quality that distinguishes a person from clouds, mountains, and "grown-ups"; it is the capacity he has to invent a purpose for himself that outweighs everything else and to which he will dedicate his life. Today we call this purpose "sacrifice"; in the past we used to call it "honor."

The essence of a person is that he *is what he isn't*. He is what he has been, and he is what he has yet to be. He is whatever lies between nothingness and being. Or, to put it simply, we might say *man is Spirit,* that sincere and marvelous creative force each one of us is vested with at birth, that force which turns a lump of flesh into a human being.

*

"Here is my secret," says the fox when it takes leave of the little prince: "It's quite simple: One sees clearly only with the heart. Anything essential is invisible to the eyes." Perhaps to the eyes, yes, but where the Spirit is concerned, if our readers are to be able to perceive something invisible, it must be personified by something that *exists* without really existing, and that is where the little prince comes into the picture. For unlike the pilot stranded in the desert, whose persona is tangible and plausible and who, were it to come down to it, could have easily been a character lifted from a Balzac novel, the little prince belongs to a whole other literary tradition. He can't be labeled or defined by any profession; he's free of any of the constraints of our existence. And that's why he alone can breathe the ineffable breath that is peculiar to man, the Spirit, into the world of grown-ups.

4. Antoine de Saint-Exupéry, "Memories of Général Chambe," in *Écrits de Guerre (Wartime Writings), 1939–1944* (Paris: Gallimard, 1982), p. 513.

5. Antoine de Saint-Exupéry, *"Lettres amicales et professionnelles,"* in *Œuvres Complètes,* vol. II, p. 1051.

The intersection of these two worlds, the visible and the invisible, is the thematic basis for *The Little Prince* and is what endows a person with his true nature. On the one hand, there is the world of *time,* with all its milestones and imperatives, and on the other, the world of *timelessness,* as embodied by the "little fellow" who never ages. Like most stories, this one begins in the visible world, within the framework of a specific event: an airplane crashed in the desert, stranding an aviator. But the story doesn't continue in this vein; it doesn't carry on with the expected description of the extrication from the calamity. Instead it "lifts off the ground," and continues in an indeterminate realm whose points of reference are vague at best. It is told with such forcefulness that it makes our eagerness to keep tabs on things destined to come to an end look ridiculous.

Time, of course, generates its own space, and this space too has a double nature: it can be measured (in miles), and yet it is infinite, even if the little prince can traverse it with the blink of an eye. Tangible, mathematical time and the space that comes with it are the realm of "grown-ups." They are of no interest to the "little fellow," who isn't even aware of them. This is why he can go from one planet to another, from one asteroid to another, as if he's playing a game in which all he has to do is decide that the chair he's sitting on is a rocket, to find himself at the other end of the universe. Here lies the virtuosity of literature: it takes playfulness for granted and showcases it with marvelous simplicity.

The fondness of "grown-ups" for *visible signs* is replaced in this story by an open-mindedness that makes it possible for someone to look at a friend's drawing and see not only the sheep inside the crate, but also that "this one is already quite sick." It is replaced by hidden meanings—as invisible as the little prince's planet— that are the constructs of the spirit and that express our sense of certainty that life indeed has a purpose, even if, without knowing it, each of us must trust whatever we can manage to come up with on that front, as each of us is condemned to living with our own understanding of the purpose of life.

We are burdened with this understanding even if, be it out of laziness, the need to conform to others,

"So, Jean-Gérard, how is it going? St. Ex." Small figure with a pickax and carrot. Drawing for Jean-Gérard Fleury.

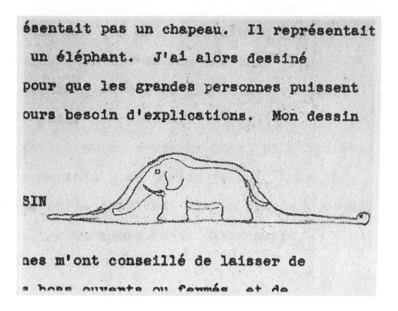

ésentait pas un chapeau. Il représentait
un éléphant. J'ai alors dessiné
pour que les grandes personnes puissent
ours besoin d'explications. Mon dessin

SIN

nes m'ont conseillé de laisser de

modesty, or sheer stupidity, we decide to believe, instead, in someone else's sense of purpose. The things of this world and of our life *are* what they *are,* for sure, but the knot that each one of us devises to bring them together within the context of our own existence is hidden, invisible, just as the destiny of a heap of bricks is in the hands of a builder who might use them for a cathedral, but might just as well use them for the walls of a prison, a hospital, a playroom, a school, or a home . . . This knot is the "hidden treasure"—and its value is in no way affected by the level of success we have with our plans, or by our failures.

The "hidden treasure" casts a light on the realities of our world. It changes a desert (desolate and empty as it is) into a space to be embraced in one's search for a well. And it changes the water from that well into something more than "merely a drink"; it makes it party to the miracle that can transform a world of rough stones—the "granite earth" the snake speaks of in the story—into the symphonic world of wind, sand, and stars. This intangible network makes it possible for us to bring things together, through our imagination, into a system that gives us a reason to live—it may be provisional and uncertain, but it is fertile and effective.

On one end of this spectrum, we have the termite mound (or the *anthill*), the mob, the masses, social issues, Karl Marx's famous "market forces," history, and everything else that aggregates individuals so that they can better function according to the rules of the universe—and, God forbid, not blossom into anything of their own accord. And on the other end, we have the individual, the only one who builds relationships, who takes on responsibilities, who works with the spirit, all of which makes him worthy of his God and makes him capable, like Him, of existing outside of things, outside of all that does not endure. And when capitalism and communism join forces to make us believe that a person's calling in life is actually "work," we have Saint-Exupéry to remind us "we have to change man, and the only way to do so is to guarantee he will have leisure."[6]

The unique thing about a termite mound is the constant marching about of the termites; they're like the comings and goings of the people who board trains without knowing where they're going, always in a mad rush and at the end of their rope. But an individual travels without ever leaving his home. "There are three things that ruin spiritual ascension," Saint-Exupéry writes in one of his letters near the end of his life: foremost of these "is the voyage itself . . ."[7] In effect, marching about takes place within a tangible space, but a voyage, as understood by the author of *The Little Prince,* is an adventure of the imagination, a spiritual game that unfolds where no mile marker could ever exist. And *The Little Prince,* one could easily imagine, is our ticket for that voyage.

✳

6. *Carnets (Notebooks)* in *Œuvres Complètes,* vol. I, p. 521.

7. "Social and professional correspondence," from Antoine de Saint-Exupéry, *Cahiers (Notebooks),* in *Œuvres Complètes,* vol. II (Paris: Gallimard, 1999), p. 1049.

The little prince with a fir tree, 1943.

The Myth of The Little Prince

OLIVIER ODAERT

Professor of twentieth-century
French literature at the Académie des
Beaux-Arts in Tournai, France

When the little prince first appears in the story to which he lends his name, he causes great surprise. The narrator tells us that when he first saw this extraordinary fellow appear out of nowhere (almost as if in answer to his appeal for a context to tell his story about the breakdown of his plane in the Sahara), he stared at him with "wide-eyed" incredulity. His disbelief has the effect of underscoring the implausibility of this encounter and invites us to take stock of all of its strangeness: "Don't forget that I was a thousand miles from any inhabited territory. Yet this little fellow seemed to be neither lost nor dying of exhaustion, hunger, or thirst; nor did he seem scared to death. There was nothing in his appearance that suggested a child lost in the middle of the desert." [1]

No doubt, when *The Little Prince* was first published in New York in 1943, its appearance also caused great surprise. For the book, which made no effort to disguise itself as anything but a fairy tale, was not only launched in the tragic context of World War II, but also broke tradition with its author's earlier work, which had been grounded in reality. His *Flight to Arras* had been part of a genre known as "literature of commitment," literature that reflects the author's belief in the idea that an artist is committed to human freedom. Published in the United States in February 1942, *Flight to Arras* told the story of the French defeat in the spring of 1940, just a few months after the outbreak of hostilities, from the point of view of a pilot who'd risked his life in the events surrounding the retreat from battle.

His writings recounted events that the author, celebrated pilot for the Aéropostale Company, had participated in. And the first pages of *The Little*

1. Antoine de Saint-Exupéry, *Le Petit Prince*, in *Œuvres Complètes*, vol. II (Paris: Gallimard, 1999), p. 238.

Prince, which are autobiographical in tone, are in keeping with this style. Nothing happens to ruffle the implicit pact of understanding that comes with this genre *until* the sudden appearance of the mysterious little fellow.

Unexpected as *The Little Prince* was, and unlike *Flight to Arras* and *Wind, Sand and Stars,* which were met with resounding success in the States, it enjoyed a more lukewarm reception. In November 1943, an American journalist who questioned why the book was not better received, suggested, "readers often don't respond well to a work from an author when it doesn't fit the image they've already formed of him."[2] And yet, looking closely at Saint-Exupéry's previous work, one can already discern the seeds of *The Little Prince;* the outline of one of the most celebrated books in the history of literature had already begun to take shape.

"I'm sorry to disturb you. I just wanted to say 'Good morning.'" *Letters to a Stranger,* Algeria, 1943–44.

THE ORIGINS OF THE TALE

Toward the end of the 1920s, during the period when he worked as a mail-delivery pilot along the Toulouse-Dakar line, Saint-Exupéry experienced numerous adventures in the Sahara. But the event most closely tied to those of the story he would go on to publish in 1943 took place in 1935, when he attempted to set the speed record for flight between Paris and Saigon. Somewhere above Egypt, he later recounted, he let himself be led astray by the "supernatural gleam" of a star that looked like one "the Magi might have seen."[3] Disoriented, he crashed into a sand dune. After several days of hopeless wandering in a state of thirst-induced hallucination, with André Prévot, his mechanic and copilot, they were rescued by a passing Bedouin who miraculously happened to cross their path.

2. Harry Binsse, "Lukewarm welcome for an acclaimed author," *Commonweal,* Nov. 19, 1943. In *Il était une fois . . . Le Petit Prince (Once upon a time there was . . . The Little Prince)* (Paris: Gallimard, 2006), Folio 4358, p. 238.

3. Antoine de Saint-Exupéry, *Terre des Hommes (Wind, Sand and Stars),* in *Œuvres Complètes,* vol. I (Paris: Gallimard, 1999), p. 242.

Drawing
from the
manuscript
of *Southern
Mail,* 1928.

The chapter of *Wind, Sand and Stars* in which the author recounts the events of this adventure is replete with elements that prefigure *The Little Prince.* Besides the obvious parallels between the circumstances in which the author found himself in Egypt and the situation in the opening pages of *The Little Prince,* several other important parallels exist between these two otherwise very different stories. The first concerns how the protagonists try to survive their ordeals and how they portray the choices they make to that end. In *Wind, Sand and Stars,* Saint-Exupéry recounts how, once they'd decided to "walk straight ahead" until they "keeled over," they took off "in defiance of all reason and all hope" heading east-north-east.[4] And in *The Little Prince,* when the strange little fellow suggests to the aviator that they set out in search of water, the aviator gestures in exasperation and says, "It is absurd looking for a well, at random, in the vastness of the desert."[5] In both cases, however, the protagonists set out on foot from the wreckage of their planes in pursuit of salvation, even if they know their decision to trek across the desert is absurd.

Another area in which the two stories are parallel is in the moral treatment of the protagonists' desperate trek through the desert. In both narratives, the perilous thirst they endure could be viewed as symbolic of man's thirst for something that might help him challenge modern life. In *Wind, Sand and Stars,* the author explains that he no longer understands

4. Ibid., p. 246.

5. Saint-Exupéry, *Le Petit Prince,* in *Œuvres Complètes,* vol. II, p. 303.

200

"these commuter train folk, these men who think they are men but that, like ants, are reduced to nothing more than the comings and goings imposed on them by some greater force they are not even aware of."[6] And in the chapter of *The Little Prince* where the little prince meets the railway switchman and asks him where all the passengers in the "brightly lit express train" are going, we see a similar sense of bewilderment: "They're not chasing anything," he answers. "They're sleeping in there, or else they're yawning."[7] The extrication from the desert both in *Wind, Sand and Stars* and *The Little Prince* takes on a strong spiritual connotation and might be seen as a *rebirth* rather than as a simple exercise in survival.

Numerous other similarities exist between the two books. In *Wind, Sand and Stars*, for example, the author describes coming across some strange burrows while wandering across the desert. He imagines that some fennec must live there, "a long-eared, carnivorous sand-fox the size of a rabbit," not at all unlike the character of the fox in *The Little Prince*. As he follows some of the animal's tracks, he refers to him as "my little fox" and imagines him "trotting blithely along at dawn."[8] He's surprised to find himself talking with the fox while it's searching for its burrow and he's sitting there "dreaming"[9] or, maybe, imagining the watercolors he'll make for the book he will someday produce.

The first outlines of the figure of the little prince exist on another level as well. Farther along in his quest for water, Saint-Exupéry will engage in a mysterious internal dialogue between the part of him that is hopeful and the part of him that seems to feel there is no more hope; between the part of him that indulges in imagination and the part that knows how to reason. One conceives of a fabulous town over the crest of the next dune, while the other tells him "You know perfectly well that is a mirage."[10] Through this dialogue, we come to understand that reverie is, above all else, a conscious choice: "Of course I know it's a mirage! [. . .] But what if I want to go after that mirage?"[11] When we stop imagining, everything is lost, both the hope and the suffering, and nothing is left of

Antoine de Saint-Exupéry and André Prévot, just before their departure for the Paris-Saigon flight, December 1935.

6. Saint-Exupéry, *Terre des Hommes* (*Wind, Sand and Stars*), in *Œuvres Complètes*, vol. II, p. 263.

7. Saint-Exupéry, *Le Petit Prince*, in *Œuvres Complètes*, vol. II, p. 301.

8. Saint-Exupéry, *Terre des Hommes* (*Wind, Sand and Stars*), in *Œuvres Complètes*, vol. II, p. 252.

9. Ibid., p. 253.

10. Ibid., p. 255.

11. Ibid.

the wanderer's dreams "but a vast parched void." [12] This is a lesson we will see again in *The Little Prince.* And, as if previewing what is to come, the author describes how, in those moments when one stands in the desert, trembling with cold, with one's scarf tied about one's neck, "everything changes into picture books, into fairy tales with cruel endings." [13]

Many of the elements of *The Little Prince* are there waiting to be lined up and marched into a story: the trek across the desert, the friendship of a fox, the internal dialogue between adult rationality and childish imagination, between the aviator and the eternal child. And of course the closing image of *Wind, Sand and Stars,* of a sleeping child described as being "like the princes we so often meet in fairy tales." [14]

The trail of inspiration for *The Little Prince* does not end here. There is also the figure of the dead child that haunts Saint-Exupéry's work from beginning to end. He is the son of Geneviève in *Southern Mail,* the son of Abraham in *The Wisdom of the Sands,* and the "Mozart that never-could-be" in *Wind, Sand and Stars.* The death, in 1917, of his cadet brother, François, undoubtedly played a part in this: it followed on the heels of the death of his father in 1904, which was partly responsible for his unwavering nostalgia. And then there's another death the author seems to have spent his life mourning: that of the romantic young man he'd once been, the one who was temporarily engaged to Louise de Vilmorin (to whom he confessed, many years after they had parted, that he had written his first novel in order to get over the heartbreak of that first love). The novel featured a character that was the incarnation of the "frail child" she had reproached him for being and whom he had sent off packing to "stumble upon a star." [15] We now know he would not remain on that star forever.

✳

THE MYTH OF THE ETERNAL CHILD

12. Ibid., p. 265.

13. Ibid., p. 262.

14. Ibid., p. 284.

15. Antoine de Saint-Exupéry, *Manon Danseuse et Autres Textes Inédits* (*Manon Ballerina and Other Unpublished Works*) (Paris: Gallimard, 2007), p. 48.

Over the past decade the number of adaptations, sequels, and re-interpretations of *The Little Prince* has been steadily increasing, and the figure of Saint-Exupéry seems to have taken on a legendary status, much like that of Don Juan or Peter Pan: free from the fetters of his original work, the author, like his hero, has lifted off from the little planet he came from to enter our collective memory and is now a source of inspiration for a new suite of stories and images. Though they may have been the product of a single author's creative genius at a specific moment in time, the book's main character and

François,
Gabrielle,
Simone, Antoine,
and Marie-
Madeleine, 1905.

his cadre—the fox, the rose, and the little planet—are now themselves sources of a new suite of stories (some more successful than others). *The Little Prince* is, in some regards, a "literary myth." So even though Saint-Exupéry may not have been aware of it, his hero rekindled a primordial image, one whose echoes haunt every mythological tradition: the image of the eternal child, or the divine child, to whom the little prince brings a fresh face and a new set of perspectives.

In their collaborative analysis of this archetype, the psychoanalyst Carl Gustav Jung and the philologist Károly Kerényi affirm that its "phantom [. . .] wanders through the mythology of every time and every culture." According to them, it has its origin in the distant past and faithfully represents undifferentiated human consciousness.[16] The divine child represents human consciousness in its totality: pure potential without morals or prejudices.

Kerényi has compared the different manifestations of this archetype in mythologies from around the world to get to the root of its fundamental characteristics: the divine child is *always* a child who has been abandoned and

16. Carl Gustav Jung, Charles Kerényi, and Paul Radin, *Le Fripon Divin (The Divine Rogue)*, translated by Arthur Reiss (Paris: Georg, 1984), p. 183. According to Jung, an undifferentiated consciousness is the consciousness of a primitive man for whom the world is a more or less fluid phenomenon within the stream of his own fantasy, where subject and object are undifferentiated and in a state of mutual interpenetration. carljungdepthpsychologysite.blog/2017/01/25/carl-jung-on-consciousness-and-the-unconscious.

then found, a child who has been confronted with great peril, but whose very weakness harbors unparalleled strength—"the *summum* of strength engendered by the *summum* of weakness."[17] This child also has the ability to instill a "mythological atmosphere that modern man 'associates with fairy tales'" wherever he goes.[18]

On the psychoanalytical side, Jung attributes a compensatory role to this child: the archetype of the eternal child is "destined to compensate for the extravagances of the conscious mind and, eventually, to correct them."[19] He represents and activates the potential that is ignored, hidden, and repressed by the conscious mind.

The relationship between the little prince and this archetype is evident: a timeless child who appears miraculously in the desert, Saint-Exupéry's character shares with his mythological precursors the ability to transform realistic-appearing fiction into a fantastic fairy tale, which is indeed what he does from the first moment he appears. His arrival on the scene, and his insistent request for a drawing of a sheep, are an invitation for the aviator to reacquaint himself with his own childhood self (the self that, for that matter, the little prince embodies). The child's sudden appearance in the middle of the Sahara is not so much a response to the urgent situation at hand, or a last-ditch effort to save the aviator from the cruel end he is likely to meet, but rather a vehicle to bring forth whatever is needed so that he might resume his "magnificent career as an artist." The mishap will force the aviator to rediscover his own power of imagination, which he'd abandoned and repressed ever since the failure of his "drawing Number One," of a boa that had swallowed an elephant, as outlined in the first chapter of the book.

In this sense, *The Little Prince* is a story about a return to an obliterated past. This idea of nostalgia is ubiquitous in Saint-Exupéry's work. It is why his lyrical writing about aviation is so unique: while other writers who wrote about the burgeoning business of aviation focused on its heroic aspects and animated their stories with accounts of pilots whose virtues were spotlighted against sunny, celestial backdrops, the author of *Night Flight* always favored nocturnal settings, and allowed his heroes' trajectories to change course, at one moment or another, toward the tranquil realm of dreams. And nothing ever disturbed this realm's tranquility except for the passage of the plane itself, which would eventually land somewhere and leave the pilot free to dream, to turn his thoughts back to his childhood home, that house that remains forever the first inalienable home of the heart.

17. Ibid., p. 118.

18. Carl Gustav Jung and Charles Kerényi, *Introduction à l'Essence de la Mythologie* (1941), translated from the German by H. E. Del Medico (Paris: Petit Bibliothèque Payot, 2001), pp. 51–52.

19. Ibid., pp. 136–37.

In *The Little Prince,* the individual's tendency to regression is represented by the opening image of the "boa constrictor swallowing a wild beast." And if it is true, as Gilbert Durand, the scholar of symbolic anthropology and mythology, has proposed, that "the boa constrictor's act of swallowing might be considered one of the culminating moments of infantile reverie," [20] it is because, face to face with this image, a child can give free rein to the ghost of *regressus ad uterum,* the comforting return to the protective maternal bosom. A number of observers have cast a disapproving eye on Saint-Exupéry's story precisely because it romanticizes this form of regression. Based on her reading of the story, for example, the psychologist Marie-Louise Von Franz concludes that the aviator embodies all the characteristics of the archetypal *puer aeternus* (eternal boy) and that these characteristics are made manifest by his lack of maturity, which, in turn, can be attributed to his unwillingness to let go of his adolescent psyche.[21] However, she concedes that, in its archetypal dimension, the symbol of the boy-king, or eternal child, also invokes "a renewal of life, spontaneity, a new potential, whether internal or external, that brings new meaning to life." [22] So, if the little prince's arrival upon the scene is an invitation to return to the past, it is also a ticket to rebirth.

✳

THE MORAL OF THE STORY

What should we make of the ambiguous ending of Saint-Exupéry's story? After eight days of unsuccessful attempts at repairing his plane, the aviator finally agrees to follow his new friend into the desert to look for a well, despite recognizing the absurdity of such an undertaking. Having unyoked himself from the imperatives of reason, he is finally able to understand the little fellow's preoccupations and to appreciate the lessons the fox has taught him. This decision will allow him to find a well that will quench both his own thirst and that of the little prince. The aviator responds to the child within, the one that invites him to embrace a more personal and soothing vision of the world. The next day, nevertheless, the little prince will decide to quit the Earth, and the story will close with a disappearing act that has all the trappings of a death, suggesting that the little prince's world is fatally irreconcilable with the reality of the aviator. The aviator, for his own part, will return to his life, having suddenly found a way to repair the engine of his plane.

But the story does not end here. For there is one last illustration, minimal and enigmatic, that consists of two brushstrokes beneath a single star. The epilogue

20. Gilbert Durand, *Les Structures Anthropologiques de l'Imaginaire* (Paris: Dunod, 2003; originally published in 1960), p. 244.

21. "In general, the man who is identified with the archetype of the *puer aeternus* remains too long in adolescent psychology." Marie-Louise Von Franz, *The Problem of the Puer Aeternus* (New York: Spring Publications, 1970).

22. Ibid., p. 7.

informs us it is a picture of what the aviator considers to be the "loveliest and the saddest landscape in the world."[23] Now, in keeping with tradition, every fairy tale must end with a moral, and *The Little Prince* is no exception, but this story is unusual in that it doesn't end so much with an edifying lesson (like the one the narrator tells us he learned when he was six), as with an invitation to contemplate this simple picture, a nearly barren space, and to consider what might have become of a sheep and a flower somewhere out there among the stars. The picture provides the perfect focal point for such contemplation. It is an invitation to read and reread *The Little Prince,* and to appreciate that what makes the closing image so hauntingly beautiful is not so much what it shows as what it *doesn't* show—*the little prince,* who we can only imagine is out there, somewhere, on his planet.

And this is precisely what the story is about: it is about surrendering oneself to the power of imagination and admitting, as the little prince and the aviator do, that "the stars are beautiful because of a flower you don't see." It is about understanding that "What makes the desert beautiful is that it hides a well somewhere."[24] And the strength of the story lies in its ability to set the reader's imagination free so that, reading it, one can dream and come to one's own conclusions about what might have happened to the little prince. The reader is afforded the same freedom as the little prince was when he went off into the stars, imagining the sheep of his dreams in the drawing he was clutching.

Many readers will likely have asked themselves why the author chose to have the little fellow ask the aviator for a drawing of a sheep, and not of something else. In traditional imagery the sheep is a symbol of sacrifice. In the book of Genesis, when Abraham is on the point of sacrificing his son Isaac to God, Isaac asks where the sacrificial lamb is. It is only after Abraham has laid his son on the sacrificial altar that he lifts his eyes and sees that God has sent a ram (another sheep) to sacrifice instead. Might it be, then, that the little prince asks the aviator for a sheep, because he doesn't want to be sacrificed, or to *go on being* sacrificed? The bittersweet ending of the story makes it impossible to answer this question. For the little prince disappears, even though his departure will disrupt the aviator's whole outlook on life, since now he can boast of having stars that can laugh, a telltale indication that he's rediscovered his childhood soul.

But the story itself answers its own question because for an aviator of Saint-Exupéry's renown, a serious man who preoccupied himself with serious matters and who was engaged in one of the largest conflicts in the history of mankind,

23. Saint-Exupéry, *Le Petit Prince,* in *Œuvres Complètes,* vol. II, p. 321.

24. Ibid., p. 303.

to lay aside the pen of the committed intellectual and pick up, instead, the watercolor brushes he had used when he was six to illustrate a fairy tale, speaks volumes about his commitment to protecting the child within, even at the risk of coming across as infantile to his audience. Like the aviator who *did* draw a sheep for the little prince, the author refused to sacrifice the child within for the sake of grown-up preoccupations. And the reader too, who despite the urgent demands of daily life chooses to set aside the time to read about an impertinent and fragile little character, will play his own role because in reading, he too, in a certain way, will be responding to the little prince's request and breathe new life into him with each subsequent reading.

*

A little prince. Undated sketch.

ADRIENNE MONNIER
French bookseller, literary critic and founder of Maison des Amis des Livres

Curiously, on re-reading *Southern Mail,* I realized, near the end, that it was a sort of foreshadowing of *The Little Prince:* the little prince, having fallen into the desert from a star, meets an aviator and then finds his way back to his own planet by letting himself be bitten by a snake. And in *Southern Mail,* the young pilot visits an old sergeant in the isolation of the desert, and his visit turns out to be "almost a token of love." He is "a lost child who comes into the desert to fill its void" and then doesn't so much die as "return to the star directly overhead."

And stars, whether they be stars toward which one aspires, stars one finds within oneself, or stars that are gilded by the golden touch of the finest writing, are everywhere in Saint-Exupéry's books.

At the end of *Night Flight,* for example, three stars appear like "deadly bait at the end of a fishing net." The aviator climbs toward them and cannot get down again.

And how can one avoid drawing the connection between the snake in *The Little Prince,* and the enemy plane in *Flight to Arras* that "spits forth its venom like a cobra?"

The little prince *is* Saint-Exupéry—the child he was and the one he continued to be in spite of grown-ups. He's the child he could have had and the one whom he undoubtedly would have wanted to have; he's the young friend who lets himself be tamed and then disappears. He is childhood itself, the world's childhood, the spiritual provision one finds over and over again in the beloved desert.

From "Saint-Exupéry et *Le Petit Prince," Fontaine,* May 1945,
reprinted in *Les Gazettes,* Collection L'Imaginaire, 1996

Cover for the first edition of *Mary Poppins,* Reynal & Hitchcock, New York, 1934.

PAMELA LYNDON TRAVERS
Australian writer and author of the Mary Poppins series
published by Reynal & Hitchcock

I cannot tell whether it is a book for children. Not that it matters, for children are like sponges. They soak into their pores the essence of any book they read, whether they understand it or not. *The Little Prince* certainly has the three essentials required by children's books. It is true in the most inward sense, it offers no explanations and it has a moral. But this particular moral attaches the book to the grown-up world rather than the nursery. To be understood it needs a heart stretched to the utmost by suffering and love, the kind of a heart that, luckily, is not often found in children . . .

But children quite naturally see with the heart, the essential is clearly visible to them. The little fox will move them simply by being a fox. They will not need his secret until they have forgotten it and have to find it again. I think, therefore, that *The Little Prince* will shine upon children with a sidewise gleam. It will strike them in some place that is not the mind and will glow there until the time comes for them to comprehend it . . .

We cannot go back to the world of childhood. We are too tall now and must stay with our own kind. But perhaps there is a way of going forward to it. Or better still of bearing it along with us; carrying the lost child in our arms so that we may measure all things in terms of that innocence . . .

From "Across the Sand Dunes to the Prince's Star,"
New York Herald Tribune Weekly Book Review, April 11, 1943

FRÉDÉRIC BEIGBEDER

French writer and literary critic;
winner of the 2003 Prix Interallié
for his novel *Windows on the World*

This story might have easily been called *In Search of Lost Childhood*. If Saint-Exupéry makes reference to serious and reasonable "grownups" so often in this story, it is precisely because his book is not addressed to children, but rather to those who think they're no longer children. Ultimately, the story is a manifesto against adulthood and all that so-called rational people represent. It is drafted so poetically and with such straightforward wisdom (Harry Potter, eat your heart out!) and feigned naiveté, that the underlying sense of offbeat humor and deeply moving melancholy are almost hidden.

One could say that Saint-Exupéry is a sort of humble version of Malraux and that the little prince is a fair-haired version of E.T., or a male version of Lewis Carroll's Alice (with the same troubling fascination for the lost paradise of childhood). Like many of the great aforementioned authors, Saint-Ex refused to grow older and, in this sense, *The Little Prince* was a premonition. Several months after its publication, the aristocrat, age forty-four, insisted on taking part in a reconnaissance mission over the Mediterranean and, like the little fellow of his story, disappeared. The wreckage of his Type J, Lockheed P 38 Lightning, which was modified into a type F5B, was found only [recently]. Rereading the end of the story—"Be kind! Don't let me go on being so sad: Send word immediately that he's come back . . ."—one realizes that *The Little Prince* is a last will and testament.

From *Dernière Inventaire Avant Liquidation*
(The Last Inventory Before Liquidation),
Grasset, 2001 (Folio 2003)

PHILIPPE DELERM

French author; his essay collection *La Première Gorgée de Bière et Autres Plaisirs Minuscules (The Small Pleasures of Life)* sold more than a million copies in France

I first became acquainted with *The Little Prince* by listening to the 33-rpm vinyl recording of Gérard Philipe and Georges Poujouly. I was told it was a beautiful story, and I believed it, but by the same token I was a little surprised that adults should show such great admiration for a story that, truth be told, I found a little simple-minded. I didn't read the book. I hadn't read it when I went to school either. But, much later, I came across it again, and I found that I still remembered many of its lines. Time passed again, and then I found that one phrase from the story had begun to stand out in my memory above all the others.

"I get something [out of it] because of the color of the wheat." Now I'm sure of it. Every bit of the poetic uniqueness of this story has been drawing me toward this one phrase all along. We all know the context: the fox wants the little prince to tame him. It tells him how wheat fields mean nothing to him, but that if the little prince will tame him, they'll always remind him of him since his hair is the color of gold, which is the same as the color of wheat. And when they are about to take leave of each other and the little prince can see how sad the fox will be now that he has been tamed, the fox reassures him by saying "I get something [out of it] because of the color of the wheat."

I understand it's fashionable in intellectual circles to look down on *The Little Prince* as being somewhat naive. So be it. And yet, no school of philosophy, no religion, has ever been as equal to the task as this book is of providing me with such a satisfying answer to the question "Why is it so that one should love one's neighbor?"

It is because one gets something [out of it] because of the color of the wheat. Our only chance of finding some meaning in our short sojourn here on Earth, in other words, is by loving someone.

From *Il était une fois . . . Le Petit Prince*
(Once upon a time there was . . . The Little Prince),
Gallimard, 2006

210

PHILIPPE FOREST

French author and professor of literature;
awarded the First-Novel Prix Femina
for *L'Enfant Éternal*

"What is one to make of the isolation of consciousness itself in a universe that has become atomized (the asteroids in space) and barren (the desert on Earth), and where there is no real chance of feeling connected with others?" This is the philosophical and existential question the little prince is confronted with in the tale to which he lends his name. The answer, as presented in the famous lesson the fox lavishes upon the little prince, is that to escape this isolation, one must learn to *tame* things; one must form emotional bonds. [. . .]

But the moral of *The Little Prince*—a moral that is at once bitter and sweet, that disarms us and turns any interpretation we might make on its head—is deeper than that. It doesn't have to do only with the emotional bond we form with something we love. No, its scope is far broader than that; in fact, it stretches the reach of that emotional bond so that it encompasses the entire universe. And, at the same time, it accepts as a given the fact that anything loved is at once possessed and lost. For only the absence of the object of our love will bring us meaning and add value to our world. [. . .] The wheat will be gold in color, the stars will be bright, and the water collected from a well will be fresh, all because, for someone, they are a reminder of a loved one. And the only way they can go on being a reminder is if they, themselves, are absent.

To fully appreciate this revelation, one must consider it in the context of the emptiness that exists within things; and one must understand that, ultimately, all things are connected: "The stars are beautiful because of a flower you don't see . . ." This void is necessary because it provides a space wherein things can connect with one another. This is what the little prince teaches us before he leaves.

From *Pilote de Guerre—L'Engagement Singulier de Saint-Exupéry*
(*Flight to Arras: A Singular Commitment*), Gallimard, 2013

THOMAS DE KONINK

Canadian philosopher and professor;
his family hosted Saint-Exupéry when de Koninck
was a child

Every man lives on his own planet. Each of us experiences the world through our own spectrum of emotional experiences, and the way we view it depends on whether we are experiencing anguish or joy. Sure, the planet we live on is the tangible one we call Earth, but, more than that, it is the personal one each of us calls home, the one we dream of and hold in our hearts, the one peopled with all those whom we love, whose presence, words, and smiles linger on even after they themselves have departed. The only planet that matters is the one we carry within, the one where we first discovered beauty, where we experienced all that is universal, and where we sensed the frailty and strength of life. It is the one where we sensed sadness, disenchantment, the nonsensical and the joyous: love and the meaning that comes with experience. "What moves me so deeply about this sleeping little prince is his loyalty to a flower—the image of a rose shining within him like the flame within a lamp, even when he's asleep . . ." [Chapter XXIV]. These lines demonstrating Saint-Exupéry's feeling on the subject very much echo those of the German poet Hölderlin, who wrote "Full of merit, yet poetically, man / Dwells on this earth."

From *Il était une fois . . . Le Petit Prince*
(*Once upon a time there was . . . The Little Prince*),
Gallimard, 2006

Appreciations

The little prince
and his scarf . . .
*Letters to a
Stranger*, Algeria,
1943–44.

QUENTIN BLAKE
British artist and member of the Légion d'Honneur;
illustrator of works by the British author Roald Dahl

I am sitting in a wicker armchair in my studio in France. In front of me I have a little book that shows the drawings that Antoine de Saint-Exupéry did while he was thinking about *Le Petit Prince* and deciding what [his character] might look like. This is something I find very interesting because sometimes people think you "invent" characters. Perhaps you do have some idea of what they are going to be like, but what really happens is that you make their acquaintance as you draw them. It's fascinating to see Saint-Exupéry drawing the look of surprise that the *petit prince* has in his eyes—and sometimes he looks almost cross. Even though he is small, he is obviously determined.

And then [there's] the scarf. I think a lot of the French like scarves, and so do I, both in real life and in my drawings. In drawings they are useful because they help to express movement. But the scarf of the *petit prince* stretches out like a flag even when he is standing still, as though blown by the intergalactic winds of the extraordinary places he finds himself. It's as though it tells us what is happening is really exciting. Brilliant.

212

MICHAEL MORPURGO
British author;
Steven Spielberg adapted Morpurgo's novel *War Horse* as a feature film

Whenever disparaging voices are raised against children's literature, I think of Antoine de Saint-Exupéry and *The Little Prince.* Here is a book for children, that is, for the child in us all, so complex and so beautiful that only the child in us can understand it. Only the light of innocence can truly illuminate this masterpiece of literature.

The Little Prince defies literary definitions because it embraces so many. Is it a short story, a novella, a prose poem, an illustrated children's novel, a work of philosophy, psychology, or politics? It is all of these and none of these. It is simply *The Little Prince.*

This simple, wondrous, visionary little story also defies all statistical superlatives: more than 200 million copies sold worldwide, translated into two hundred languages, the most read and translated book ever written by a Frenchman—it could hardly have been written by anyone else—[and] so widely read and loved that it has been adopted by numerous nationalities as their own. Shakespeare achieves this universal appeal with dozens of plays. Saint-Exupéry does it with one little story. Somehow *The Little Prince* resonates across cultures, religions, and races—it is indeed a book for our times. The story seems oblivious to the passing of the years, gathering new admirers all the time, by the millions.

So why this miraculous longevity, this unique universal appeal? Perhaps the genius of the story is that it is unfathomable. It is a dream we spend the rest of our lives trying to interpret. We read it again and again. The simplicity of the story is an illusion of course, simply the framework for the complexity of the philosophical ideas it explores. It is a perfect fusion, a marriage of mirage and miracle, marvel, and mystery.

PEF (PIERRE ELIE FERRIER)
French author and illustrator; creator of Prince de Motordu

By the time I came to know *The Little Prince* it was too late. What [its author] and I shared was our obsession with airplanes. But I'm certain now that the little prince was there in my Breguet XIV, and that he'd reserved a seat for the days yet to come when life would be better than it was in 1916. This yellow biplane had started out life as a bomber and was subsequently bought by the airline Latécoère, who modified it for use as a mail carrier. In this capacity, it delivered stories, contracts, and, no doubt, many a love letter to Morocco and South America. And it was this type of plane that Saint-Exupéry, post carrier and airman in a new war (which, it is said, was fought for economic reasons), piloted between brutal reality and celestial escape routes until, pushed to the breaking point, he gave birth to the little prince.

HAYAO MIYAZAKI
Japanese film director and cofounder of Studio Ghibli;
his Academy Award–winning animated film *Spirited Away* (2001)
is the highest-grossing film in Japanese history

To me, Saint-Exupéry's life is part of an inviolable province. A diamond, he disappeared into the sea before being cut. But neither the customs nor the upheavals of an era can cause a diamond to lose its brilliance, even if it is in the rough. *Wind, Sand and Stars,* which celebrates the era of the early years he spent working for both the now bygone mail delivery company Aéropostale and for the nobility of mankind, is proof of this. For even after all these years it has lost none of its splendor.

In addition to being a writer, Saint-Exupéry was also [of course] an aviator who, having been forced to land his plane on our star, had already had a brush with death before he eventually disappeared. If, in the end, he survived, it was so that he could go on to write *Wind, Sand and Stars* and *The Little Prince.* Once he'd accomplished this, what other reason would he have to go on living? He'd tried before to take off from our star, and after several failed attempts, several injuries, he finally managed to turn this desire into reality, in the Mediterranean.

From Antoine de Saint-Exupéry, *Drawings*, Gallimard, 2006

Two drawings by Saint-Exupéry,
late 1930s.

* *

MARK OSBORNE
American film director, writer, and animator;
director of *The Little Prince* animated movie (2015)

In the text, the aviator says that he didn't want his book to be taken lightly, and it is clear this is Antoine de Saint-Exupéry speaking directly to us, asking us as gently as possible to read very carefully and not to brush this story off as merely a book for kids. It is so delicately crafted to be so much more than that, speaking to every age that exists within us all. If you know the book, regardless of what age it entered your life, chances are good that you do not take it lightly. It stays with you and becomes a permanent part of your universe, as it has forever become a part of mine. I just hope I don't ever grow up too much to forget it.

January 2013

ADAM GOPNIK
American author and staff writer for *The New Yorker*

The men the Prince meets on his journey to Earth are all men who have, in Bloch's sense, been reduced to functions. The Businessman, the Astronomer, even the poor Lamplighter, have become their occupations, and gone blind to the stars. It is, again, the essential movement we find in Camus, only in *The Little Prince* it is shown to us as comic fable rather than realistic novel. The world conspires to make us blind to its own workings; our real work is to see the world again.

From "The Strange Triumph of *The Little Prince*,"
The New Yorker, April 29, 2015

STACY SCHIFF
American biographer and author of *Saint-Exupéry: A Biography*

He neither reinvented nor muddied the past. He was not untruthful. He put a gloss on things, but he lived too for that gloss, for a quixotism that would be his undoing. The fashion in which he shaped the events he faithfully reported ultimately tells us as much about him as do the events themselves.

From *Saint-Exupéry: A Biography*, Alfred A. Knopf, 1994

* *

JOANN SFAR

French comic artist, writer, and film director;
illustrator of *The Little Prince* graphic novel adaptation (2010)

The little prince is not a child. If he were, it would be too sad because, in the end, he dies. This is a matter of debate, of course, and one we mull over time after time, whenever we are out of sorts. Then we put it to rest, only to revisit it again and again. *The Little Prince* presents a unique portrayal of transcendence, because it never once stops asking us to gaze up into the heavens, not so much to look for Jesus or anything like that, but so that, in doing so, we might be reminded of a certain time, a certain someone. For when we look at things, a field of wheat, or the stars, for example, we do so to revive our best memories. And how do we revive them? Through drawings, of course: for drawings are the most poetic repository of what the world has to offer. From beginning to end, this is what *The Little Prince* is all about. How can it be that I, who have dedicated my whole life to drawing, who have stared up at the sky without ever expecting to see anything, should have found there a reason to be happy on Earth? And, having done so, how could I ever turn my back on this book now? It says everything I've ever wanted to say since I started telling stories.

There are certain rules I always try to abide by while drawing cartoons, and now I've broken every single one of them. Usually, for example, every time I move on to a new page, I begin a new chapter. But when I worked on the comic adaptation of *The Little Prince,* I did the opposite: I kept going and going. And usually, when I realize a story I am telling is becoming too sad, I throw in a wisecrack. But Saint-Exupéry had no qualms about venturing into the depths of melancholy when he wrote *The Little Prince,* so I too try to chart my way within it: I stay with the character when he cries, and I stay with him when he has stopped crying. I take my time. I guess you could say I am "more Japanese" than usual: I aim for *manga,* for something reminiscent of Japanese cinema, of its way of stretching time out, à la Jasugirō Ozu. The only way to avoid coming across as mawkish, with this book, is to never underestimate the gloom of what one is telling.

The Little Prince does not shy away from the truth and treats the subject of death openly. In my opinion, one shouldn't make books unless they serve a purpose. The books of Roald Dahl, Tomi Ungerer, and Maurice Sendak serve a purpose. And I like them more than most books for adults that are thicker, but boring.

From evene.fr, September 16, 2008

The little prince as seen by Joann Sfar; unpublished drawings.

A Brief Biography

"I was wrong to grow older. Pity. I was so happy as a child."

— *Flight to Arras*

The legendary author and aviator Antoine de Saint-Exupéry created some of the most poetic and true-hearted stories of the past century, leaving behind a prolific legacy that continues to resonate with readers young and old. Born a French aristocrat in 1900 in Lyon, France, the son of a wealthy, industrious count, Saint-Exupéry enjoyed luxury and privilege during his childhood. A wide-eyed dreamer even as a young boy, Antoine, or "Tonio," as he was called by his friends and family, yearned to touch the sky and discharge his restless nature. With his four playful siblings and storytelling mother, this happy time was the source of many of Saint-Exupéry's fondest memories and of the nostalgia that would permeate his work.

Sadly, periods of sorrow were interwoven with Saint-Exupéry's fond recollections. Tragedy struck his life early—his father died before Saint-Exupéry was four years old, leaving the family without the father's business to rely on, and without guidance. They moved to live with a relative in the southeast of France, at Saint-Maurice-de-Rémens in Ain, La Mole, Provence, where Saint-Exupéry and his remaining family experienced

220

✱ ✱

a mostly idyllic and carefree lifestyle. These cherished recollections in the magnificent chateau in the south of France would find their way into his books. Eventually they moved to Le Mans, the home of Saint-Exupéry's grandfather, where coincidentally, one of the Wright brothers had recently visited to show the French aviators his astounding flying techniques in the legendary Wright Flyer. However, devastating loss struck the family again as Saint-Exupéry's younger brother, François, died of rheumatic fever at age fifteen while at school. This loss affected Saint-Exupéry greatly — the experience would perhaps be reflected in the melancholy departure of the little prince. "It wasn't such a heavy body . . ."

Saint-Exupéry flew for the first time at twelve years of age and he immediately became determined to be a pilot. Having spread his wings, he turned his mind forever to the sky and the stars beyond. After studying architecture at the École des Beaux-Arts, he served in the military as a pilot. Although he took various jobs afterward, he eventually returned to his passion and became a pilot for Aéropostale, a private airline flying mail from France to Senegal. In 1927, while working

in southern Morocco, Saint-Exupéry wrote his first book, a memoir called *Southern Mail*. In 1931, he published his first novel, *Night Flight,* which won instant success and the prestigious Prix Femina. His work for Aéropostale took him to South America, where he met his future wife, Consuelo Suncín de Sandoval. Unique, highly intelligent, and fiercely independent, the daughter of a wealthy Salvadoran landowner and widow of the

"One's suffering disappears when one lets oneself go, when one yields — even to sadness."

— *Southern Mail*

221

Argentinian ambassador to France, Consuelo connected with Saint-Exupéry immediately—bonding over a shared language, a passion for literature, and their similar restless spirits. Over the years, their marriage was famously stormy. Their relationship was immortalized in the complex yet affectionate bond between the little prince and his beloved rose.

Love of flight consumed Saint-Exupéry's life, and embedded itself in his work. In 1935, he attempted to break the speed record for flying from Paris to Saigon. But his plane crashed in the Sahara, and with only one day's worth of water, he and his copilot wandered through the dunes for more than three days. This near-death experience would provide the character and setting for many of his books, including the stranded aviator in *The Little Prince*. He was seriously injured in a second plane crash, this time as he tried to fly between New York City and Tierra del Fuego, Argentina, in 1938. The crash resulted in a long convalescence in New York. Saint-Exupéry's second novel, *Wind, Sand and Stars,* was published in 1939 and won the Grand Prix du Roman of the Académie française and, in the United States, the National Book Award: a promise of what was to come for Saint-Exupéry's career in the States.

At the beginning of World War II, Saint-Exupéry flew reconnaissance missions for France. With the fall of France to the Germans in 1940, the author returned to New York to solicit aid for his suffering homeland. He drew on his wartime experiences to write *Flight to Arras* and *Letter to a Hostage,* both published in 1942. This

"It is always in the midst, in the epicenter, of your troubles that you find serenity."

—*Wartime Writings, 1939–1944*

222

> **"I have in mind the far-flung glory of the night when one stands on the heights, alone and shivering, amongst the stars."**
>
> — *The Wisdom of the Sands*

period of self-imposed exile sank the author into depression; he regretted remaining apart from the action. It was in this state of seclusion on Long Island that he wrote his most famous work: *The Little Prince*.

Late in 1943, Saint-Exupéry rejoined his squadron in northern Africa. Though forbidden to fly because of complications from his crashes, Saint-Exupéry insisted on taking a mission. On July 31, 1944, he set out from Borgo, Corsica, to fly over occupied France. He never returned. His plane was shot down by German combatants, and his body was never found. The wreckage of his plane was not located until many years later, when an ID bracelet was found bearing only his name and the address of his New York publisher—the first

to publish his final, most famous, and arguably most profound work of literature, *The Little Prince*. Although *The Little Prince* was published just a year before his death, and he never knew the enormous impact it would have on the world, the New York publisher's address on the ID bracelet underscores the deep connection Saint-Exupéry shared with his golden-haired alter ego—who also had his eyes set on the stars.

Throughout his life, Saint-Exupéry longed for a return to childhood, influenced by the isolation from his home country during its defeat and the stress of the war surrounding him. With perhaps both his idealized childhood and the immediate grave historical circumstances in mind, he changed the dedication of the book at the last minute. Instead of his wife, Consuelo, the tempestuous rose in *The Little Prince* and his original planned dedicatee, he chose his close friend Léon Werth, a fellow Frenchman persecuted for his Jewish faith and pacifist political beliefs, who had been suffering in France at the time. Saint-Exupéry wrote the dedication specifically to Werth "when he was a little boy," asking children to forgive him for "dedicating this book to a grown-up," and explained that "All grown-ups were children first. (But few of them remember it.)" Rooted in hopeful nostalgia and dreaming of better times than the war-stricken era in which he lived, Antoine de Saint-Exupéry shared with the world the brilliant mind of an intellectual dreamer, an existentialist philosopher with a hope for a return to innocence and compassion, and ultimately, a storyteller in flight.

"Life has taught us that love does not consist in gazing at each other but in looking outward together in the same direction."

—*Wind, Sand and Stars*